WATSON'S

AFGHAN

ADVENTURE

Kieran McMullen

Paperback ISBN 978-1-907685-93-4
ePub ISBN 978-1-907685-94-1
Mobipocket/Kindle ISBN 978-1-907685-95-8

Published in the UK by MX Publishing
335 Princess Park Manor, Royal Drive,
London, N11 3GX
www.mxpublishing.co.uk

Cover design by www.staunch.com

To Helen, my best friend.

Chapter 1

It had been a long but beneficial day. The late April days in London had been clear and pleasant and in the parks at least, the smell of spring was wonderful.

Holmes had concluded two rather interesting cases in the last weeks. One I had titled "The Case of the Hansom Horse" and the other "The Adventure of the Locked Tantalus". Should Holmes approve, I would put them aside for a year or two before offering them to Mr Doyle for publication.

So here I was, strolling home, sunshine, a day of rounds, my lunch at the club and now to Baker Street and a relaxing evening. Life was good.

As I approached 221, I noticed a hansom cab pulling away from the kerb and wondered if we had had a visitor in my absence. With a quickened step, I advanced to the door and trotted up the seventeen steps to our sitting room. As I entered, I saw Holmes by the bow window, pipe in hand and looking most contemplative.

"Holmes," I said as I laid down my bag and hat, "Have we had a visitor?"

"Ah Watson," said he turning toward me and moving to his favourite chair. "Yes, we or actually you, have had a visitor."

"I? And who would that have been?"

"Actually, it was your old orderly, Murray." He said, sitting and propping his feet on the fender of the cold fireplace.

"I should greatly like to have seen him. Is he to be in London for a time? Where is he staying?"

"I'm afraid you've missed him, Watson. He is on his way to the train, thence to Liverpool and finally to America. I understand he is to live with his daughter and her husband in a town called Guthrie in the Indian Territory of all places. They evidently are in some kind of a mercantile business and invited him to live with them and the grandchildren now that his wife has passed."

Suddenly, my happy mood had been rained on. Feeling irritated with myself for having dawdled at the club, I sat in my chair on the other side of the fireplace. "Well I'm greatly sorry to have missed him. He and I had more than one adventure together and I'll always be in his debt. It's sad to think I'll probably never see him again."

Holmes leant forward in his chair and retrieved his Persian slipper. Filling his old clay with tobacco, he leaned back and smiled. "He did leave you something to remember him by," said Holmes. "Over there on the table, a white cardboard box. Murray said you would understand its contents. He also said he will be forever grateful to you. He did not explain why and I did not press him for an explanation."

Rising, I went to the table upon which lay a white cardboard box about six inches square, two inches high, tied with twine and unmarked. It rattled slightly when I picked it up. I returned with it to my chair and cutting the string with my pocketknife, I heard Holmes chuckle. "Preserving the knot as evidence, Watson?" I had to smile.

"I suppose you have had an effect on my habits, Holmes. But it's really just faster to cut it."

Leaning back, I opened the box. I don't know what the look on my face was but my reaction evidently startled Holmes. "Watson" he said, "Are you all right? Can I help with something, old friend?" Closing the lid on the box, I stood and leaning on the mantel, looked into the cold space. "No Holmes, I'm quite fine. It's just that a sudden flood of emotions seemed to overwhelm me. Sorry."

"No need to apologize, Watson. Would you care for a whiskey?"

"Quite right, Holmes, I would."

A short whiskey, a deep breath and I felt myself again.

"Holmes," I said, "How do you feel about dinner at Simpson's tonight? My treat."

"Excellent, Watson, we deserve a night out. I'll inform Mrs Hudson."

We enjoyed an excellent leisurely dinner and it was near eleven when we returned to Baker Street. I was again feeling all was well with the world and had even enjoyed Holmes' constant one-sided discussion on the merits of the horseless carriage and its positive effect on the London environment. As we sat with a last evening brandy, I turned to Holmes, "I suppose you have deduced, by now, the contents of the package left me by Murray."

"No, other than it contained some memento of your time together in Afghanistan, I have no idea."

"Well, let me show you and see what you can deduce. I can believe that is should be fairly easy for you."

Taking the package from the mantle, I handed it to Holmes who put it on the edge of his chair while finishing lighting his pipe. The pipe lit, he opened the box and examined its contents. Rising, he moved to the table and one by one, removed the contents: one glass phial containing two bullets, a ruby of approximately 5 carats and a medal with a likeness of St. Peters Basilica on the reverse with the date of 1880 and on the obverse a likeness of Pope Gregory XVI and subscribed "John H. Watson".

For the first time, in a long time, I saw a quizzical look on Holmes' face.

"Well Holmes, what do you make of it?"

"Some of this is obvious of course, but some is curious." He said. Picking up the phial, he opened it and placed the two bullets on the table and taking up his magnifying glass, he examined them thoroughly. The ruby was next to be examined and lastly the Papal medal. Sitting at the table, he once again picked up the two bullets.

"I am of the opinion that these two bullets make my friend out to be a liar."

"Holmes!" I cried.

"These two bullets are undoubtedly the two that came from your shoulder and your leg. Why else would Murray have saved them all these years? Neither, however, was fired from a Jizail. This one here was fired from a Snider rifle." He said. "A Jizail, while sometimes rifled, is usually a smooth bore musket, and in either case will be about .56 to .79 calibres. This bullet is a .577 of about 480g with a hollow cavity, I believe it is called a Metford and it was fired by a weapon with five grooves, therefore a Snider short rifle or carbine."

Picking up the other bullet, Holmes continued, "This bullet is a pistol bullet. Probably from an Enfield Mark I. The .476 calibre and rifling are very distinctive. Neither bullet, however," he said, dropping the bullets in the phial," is from a Jizail. And since you have always contended that you were wounded by a Jizail bullet, you have obviously lied. For what purpose I don't know, but I assume they have something to do with this ruby and an award to John H. Watson from the Roman Pope."

I was mortified and ashamed. "Yes, Holmes, I have lied to you. Those are the bullets from my wounds and while there was plenty of fighting involved, only one of the wounds ever came from an Afghan fighter. Perhaps it is time that you at least knew what really happened in Afghanistan."

Chapter 2

Holmes walked back to the sideboard and poured two more brandies. "You know that that is not necessary, Watson. Whatever the cause, I know that you are a man of honour and would have done nothing immoral. Illegal perhaps, as you have shared a few less than legal moments with me. Whatever happened, it was in a good cause."

"Thank you, Holmes." I replied. "But I really would like to tell you what those items represent. I'm afraid to do so though might be a bit lengthy in the telling."

"As you know, Watson, we have no cases at the present and I, for one, am not tired and you have always been fairly closed-mouthed about the details of your Army service. I see no reason to not tell your tale right now."

"I'm afraid, Holmes, that it starts back in the days of my youth. As you know, I was born in August of '52 in Hampshire. Both of my parents were Scotch Presbyterian. Being the second son, and my older brother already named after my father, that is Henry Watson, Jr., I was named for my father's first cousin, John Watson, who was serving in the Bombay Army. He and my father had been inseparable as children. My middle name, Hamish, was my mother's father's name. All this may sound irrelevant, but it all ties into what happened to me in Afghanistan."

"Mother died when I was not quite two. In fact, it was June 24th, 1854. Father was a Railroad Construction Engineer and had been given an opportunity to work on the building of the Sydney railroad. So in August of '54, he packed up my brother and I and a nanny by the name of Eileen Duffy and off we went to Australia. There were no close relatives on my mother's or father's sides of the family living, so there was nothing to hold us here in England.

"Father completed his work on the Sydney railroad when it was opened on September 26, 1855. From then on it was a series of railroad camps across different parts of Australia and finally in the summer of 1857, two things happened. First, father took a position as Railroad Inspector for the Crown and second, as these things will happen, he married Miss Duffy, or Miss Eileen as we boys called her.

"She was a wonderful woman and Henry and I thought the world of her. She insisted that we continue to call her Miss Eileen in deference to our deceased mother. Miss Eileen not only saw to our physical needs and education, she now saw to our religious education. Father, although nominally Presbyterian, was truly an agnostic. He had little use for organized religion. Miss Eileen however was a devout Catholic and being a woman, knew how to bend her husband's will to hers. So it was that Mrs Eileen Watson and sons became regular members of the St. Mary's Catholic Church. Henry and I made our first communion two years later.

"It was also in '57 that my father and his cousin John began a communication that lasted until the death of my father. I also started corresponding with my namesake and he quickly became my hero. Lt. John Watson of the 1st Punjab Cavalry won the Victoria Cross at Lucknow during the Sepoy Mutiny.

"I was thrilled to hear of his gallant charge against a Ressaldar and six enemy sowars. Firing his pistol at a distance of three feet, the Ressaldar missed and Lt. Watson ran him through with his sabre and dismounted him. The Ressaldar was not finished though and with his tulwar drawn, he and his six sowars assaulted Cousin John anew. Lt. Watson defended himself until his own men could arrive and together, they vanquished the entire rebel company. Cousin John received Sabre or Tulwar cuts to the head, his left arm, his right arm (which was temporarily disabled), a bullet through his coat and a sabre cut to his leg which left him somewhat lame for awhile.

"Here was adventure for a boy to lust after. So now I knew what the future held, the Army. As I grew, I stayed in contact with Cousin John. I relished his every letter. His adventures in the mutiny, his raising of the 4th Sikh Irregular Cavalry (Watson's Horse) in '58, the Umbryla Expedition in '63, it was all a bright, shining adventure.

"Henry and I spent our days being tutored by Miss Eileen, occasionally traveling with father on a railroad inspection, exploring the Outback, learning to shoot and ride and pretending to be the conquering British soldiers in our games. This happy state lasted until my thirteenth year.

"Typhoid came in the spring of that year and with it, the death of my only mother I had really known. I watched the progress of the disease as it took her, the chills, sweating, pain, headache, fever and diarrhoea. In those days, it was called enteric fever and was treated with opiates for the diarrhoea, hot poultices for the abdominal pain, cold water sprays for the fever and turpentine by mouth for the internal ulcers.

"By the third week of her suffering, I was convinced there had to be some other treatment. I was able to find a paper by a Dr Joseph Bell of Glasgow, who as early as 1860, was successfully using silver nitrate to treat typhoid. But who would listen to a 13 year old boy anyway? And so we lost her. My only consolation was that she had seen me confirmed in the Roman Catholic faith before she died.

"I now had two missions in life. I would devote myself to medicine and the Army.

As had happened in '54, it was time for the Watson family to move on. I was sent to England to Wellington College in Hampshire. Henry however stayed with father. Henry was already 17 and knew he wanted to be a Railroad Construction Engineer. So as I sailed for England, Henry and father sailed for San Francisco and work on the expanding railroad system in America, booming with the end of the American Civil War.

"Life at Wellington took some getting used to. I quickly learned how alone I was in the world. With the exception of an occasional letter from Henry or Cousin John, I was on my own. As you know, there were hard lesson to be learned, but I found that my outdoor life had made me capable of defending myself and my education thus far had stood me in good stead. The one thing I did learn quickly was to keep my Catholicism and my opinions on the Irish Question to myself.

"Suffice it to say that I did well at my studies and excelled in athletics. I also kept up my correspondence with Cousin John. I continued to thrill at his adventures and took great pride in his receiving command of the Central India Horse in '71.

"In '72, I entered the University of London Medical School and of course worked at St. Bart's. Outside of the classroom, rugby was my life. All in all, things were good. In '74, I heard that Dr Joseph Bell was teaching at Edinburgh University and since I had a great desire to meet him, I spent a year there before returning to London. Actually Holmes, you and he are very kindred spirits. He is still there and you should meet him."

"I'm quite aware of Dr Bell and his techniques, which I agree, are much like my own," Said Holmes. "Forgive me while I refill my pipe. Go on, please. This is most interesting."

"Well" said I quite pleased that Holmes should show an interest in my history, "I returned to the University and received my Doctorate in June of '78. It was at that time that Cousin John sent me notice that he had been dispatched to Malta in command of all the Indian Cavalry. But he also wrote of the touchy situation in India on the Afghanistan border. He was convinced of an imminent war on the border and urged me to apply directly for a position with a regiment already in country. This I did. Cousin John recommended the 5th Regiment of Foot, now called the 5th Fusiliers or the Northumberland Regiment. Their nickname was the Fighting 5th.

"Everything seemed to be falling in place as far as my career. So upon leaving the University in

June, I reported to Netley for the School of the Army Surgeons and it was there that I first fell in love.

Chapter 3

Netley was not a challenging course. It amounted to four things: doctors needed to be competent (and few were), get their own men organized, get the Commanders to listen about sanitation and finally, make sure you had adequate supplies. So, for five months, I was to be as sixes and sevens, not really knowing what to do with myself, while waiting to deploy.

I decided to fill my time with a personal study of military medical issues but still had much time for my new club and one of my favourite sports, horseracing. I know Holmes, I still enjoy it too much. But at the time, besides my pay, there was still a stipend from father in America. It was on one of my track days that I met a lovely young lady named Violet Enderby. But I get ahead of myself.

I had been to the Grand National that April and had failed to place my money on Shifnal and was therefore down a bit on my funds. But in June, I was feeling good and decided to go ahead and attend the Epson Derby to celebrate my new career. It proved a most interesting day. It was there I met three people who would forever impact my life. I was just about to place a modest wager with a bookmaker when I noticed the most lovely lady walking on the arm of a man I assumed to be her father or guardian. She was about 5'2", willowy, with beautiful golden blonde hair and hazel eyes. She wore summer dress of light green with a broad brimmed hat and a parasol of matching material. Her escort wore the uniform of a Colonel of the Indian

Army. It was as they strolled by that I saw this lovely creature look my way. She smiled, nodded her head and walked on. I stood there speechless and wondering how to make her acquaintance. It was then I heard a voice at shoulder, "Give it up Old Boy. Nobody gets to meet Miss Violet."

Spinning around on my heels, I looked into the smiling faces of two young men of about my age. One put out his hand and said, "Lt. Sutter Sturt, 5th Fusiliers and the grinning Irishman next to me is Lt. Arthur McMullen of the 18th Bengal Cavalry. And the delightful creature you were admiring is Violet Enderby, daughter of the most pompous ass of a Colonel in the Indian Army. No one is good enough for his daughter."

"John Watson" I said shaking hands with both, "And delighted to meet you. I've just been assigned Assistant Surgeon with the 5th."

"Well all the better to save a fellow from certain disappointment" said Sturt. "You could have ended up like Arty here, broken heart, poorer and on the run from an angry Colonel." At this remark, the two started into a fit of laughter.

Placing his arm around my shoulder and walking toward the rail, Sturt asked if I had already placed my wager. "No." I replied. "I need to get one down quickly."

"Well" replied Sturt. "Arty and I were just about to pool our modest sum. Would you care to go in with us? Mr Cavalry claims to have a sure fire system to pick the winner."

"I've no objection as long as he's betting on Sefton."

The two laughed again and arm in arm we were off to make the wager. That night we celebrated our win at the pavilion dance. It was here that I was introduced to Miss Enderby.

The pavilion dance was a gay affair and McMullen, Sturt and I were having a wonderful time. The two of them were telling me their stories of India, and I was trying to sort truth from fiction. We danced with numerous young ladies and drank our fill.

It was about halfway through the evening that we heard a commotion coming from a far corner of the pavilion. It was followed by a call from the bandleader asking for a doctor. I immediately responded and found an elderly lady lying unconscious on the floor surrounded by people.

"Sturt! Arty! Keep these people back, please!"

The two moved the crowd back but one beautiful lady stayed, kneeling, holding the hand of the stricken woman. Miss Enderby. "Are you a doctor?" she asked.

"Yes, Miss", I replied.

"This is my great aunt; she was standing one minute and the next she was on the floor."

"Does she have any condition I should know of?"

"No" she replied. "She is quite healthy. I can't imagine what's happened."

I quickly examined the woman and as I did, she stirred slightly. "She's only fainted" I said. "A little air and some water and she'll be fine. Is there somewhere we can take her?"

"There is a lounge just off the patio" piped up a waiter who was standing by.

We moved the lady to the lounge and the crowd went back to its business of revelry.

Having deposited the lady on a chaise lounge, we commenced rubbing her arms and she soon came round. As her eyes opened, she suddenly sat upright. "Oh, my dear! What has happened?"

Tears welled up in her eyes. "Oh! I'm so embarrassed! Violet, help me up."

"I really wouldn't advise that, Madam. You really need to just sit and relax awhile. Doctor's orders." I smiled and patted her hand.

"You do what the doctor says, Aunt Katherine. I'll stay with you. It was getting rather heated in the pavilion and it's so much cooler here."

Turning to me, she said, "I want to thank you, Doctor."

"Really" I smiled, "It was no problem. Happy to help."

At this point, Sturt stepped forward. While looking at Miss Enderby, I had completely forgotten the presence of others in the room.

"Allow me to do the introductions. Miss Violet Enderby, let me present Dr John Watson of the 5th Fusiliers. And now, if you'll excuse us, Lt. McMullen and I will retire, happy to help." Smiling, he turned and grabbing Arty by the elbow, the two of them left for the bar.

"So, you're friends with Lieutenants McMullen and Sturt?"

"Yes, well, we just met today but they seem fine fellows."

"They are. I know both of them from India. They were assigned to general staff for a short time with my father, Colonel Enderby."

"Violet," called her aunt, "some more water, please."

"I best attend to my Aunt Katherine. But once again, thank you Doctor. Perhaps we'll see each other again." Violet extended her hand and taking it, I bowed.

"It will be my pleasure." I said and as I walked out, I was nearly bowled over by the form of Colonel Enderby rushing into the room.

"Was that Lt. McMullen I saw coming out of this room?" he stormed.

"Father, he was just helping with Aunt Katherine," Said Violet.

"I'll thank him not to help with anybody in this family, and who are you, Sir?"

"Assistant Surgeon Watson, Sir. Like the Lieutenant, just helping." I said, the blood rushing to my face.

"Well we appreciate your assistance" he blustered, "but we'll take it from here. Dismissed." And turning, he walked toward Aunt Katherine. Stunned, I drew myself up to attention, "You're welcome, Sir, and good night." I turned about and left to join the others at the bar.

"Get on well with the old man?" smirked Sturt as I approached. "Have a whiskey.'

"What a pompous ass!" I spit out. "No gratitude."

"That's just his way of saying he cares" laughed Arty. "Now, what about next week? Do we roll our winnings over?"

I hesitated for only a moment. "I'll be here if you both will."

"Then it's settled. We'll see if the combined knowledge of Dr Tout and Mr Cavalry can pick us another winner," chuckled Sturt.

So the following week we met again, this time for the Oak Stakes. It was much the same as the week before, and Arty and I studied the horses. Arty really was a sound judge of horse flesh and he and I finally agreed on a young filly named Jannette. The Oaks, of course, was for three year old fillies only.

As we walked about the track that fine day, you know who we saw, once again, on the arm of her father. The difference now being I had been introduced.

"Good Afternoon, Sir, Miss. What a beautiful day for racing. I do hope your good Aunt is doing well."

Miss Enderby smiled, "Quite well thanks to you, Doctor. Isn't she, Father?"

"Yes, quite well, quite well. Hope you're not looking for new clients, young man" huffed the Colonel.

"No Sir. Just enjoying the day. Will I see you at the pavilion later?" I said, smiling back at Miss Enderby.

"Perhaps, young man" scowled the Colonel. "Perhaps. Well come along Violet. Time we got along. Oh, and thank you again young man for your help last week."

With that they went off into the crowd. "That didn't go too badly" I said, turning to where Arty had stood. There was no one there. I looked all about and saw neither Sutter nor Arty until I moved up to the track.

"John, over here" called the voice of Sutter. "Go alright with the old codger?"

"I believe so but you two certainly disappeared quickly!"

"Only for the best" laughed Arty. "Now to the bar, we have time for one before the race."

The day went well for us. We bet individually on the early races and while Arty and I were better than even, Sutter was down not an inconsiderable amount. The Oaks went as we hoped and Jannette increased our pool of funds quite well. That evening, we adjourned to the pavilion to enjoy some of our winnings having agreed to take ten per cent for ourselves and place the rest on the St. Leger Stakes in September. Arty would hold our winnings until then.

It was another gay night and I looked forward to hopefully seeing Miss Enderby again. I was not to be disappointed. It was "Aunt Katherine" I found first. Having left my companions at the bar, I was wandering the pavilion when I heard above the throng, "Doctor. Doctor Watson, over here." As I looked toward the voice, I saw Katherine Enderby waving a handkerchief, surrounded by her friends of a like age. I smiled and went over to her.

"Not feeling ill tonight, are we Miss Enderby?"

"Please, please Doctor, you must call me Aunt Katherine, everyone does."

"Of course, Aunt Katherine" I grinned.

"I was so hoping I'd see you so I could thank you properly for your help last week."

"It was nothing really, happy to help."

"Now don't be modest, dear boy. I was just telling the girls what a fine doctor you are."

I smiled round at the "girls" and wondered if any of them was less than sixty. "Is the other Miss Enderby here tonight?" I asked.

"Why dear boy, of course. And you shall dance with her. Now where has she gone? Oh yes, over there with her father. Violet! Oh Violet" she called. "Here's that wonderful Doctor Watson. He so much wants to dance with you, don't you Doctor?"

Miss Enderby and I both grinned with embarrassment and took to the floor to avoid more attention. She and I danced until late; she was a startling woman, beautiful, intelligent, and courteous. She had a way of looking at you that made you feel special. As the night came to an end, Violet and I were lost in conversation.

"Violet, it's time to go dear." It was Aunt Katherine. Colonel Enderby stood next to her, quite a formidable figure with a scowl under his military moustache.

"Now, Doctor Watson, I've been talking to the Colonel and you must come visit us at the Hurling House. It's all decided. Two weeks from now, we won't take no for an answer" bubbled Aunt Katherine.

"Aunt Katherine, no one could refuse you anything. I'd be delighted."

The Colonel continued to scowl as I said my goodnights and went in search of my compatriots.

Two weeks later, I had the most wonderful weekend. For the most part, the Colonel kept to himself while I and Violet (and of course Aunt Katherine) had a wonderful time. In fact, the summer and early fall passed this way and I became a frequent guest.

Other things were happening that summer too. The undersea cable and two cross continent cables gave three telegraph routes between India and England. The Russians had opened relations with Amir Sher Ali Khan in Kabul in 1877. When we had asked for representation, the Amir refused us. In '78, the Amir signed a treaty with the Russians and moved large numbers of his Afghan troops to the border of the Northwest Frontier. Everyone knew there would be war and troop movements began. Cousin John commanded a large portion of native troops. He let me know that now was the time to get to my unit, yet I chaffed under the constraints of a slow, methodical course for Army surgeons and knew it would be end of November before we would ever set sail.

In September, McMullen, Sturt and I met in Doncaster for the St. Leger Stakes. You could tell that we all strained to be away to India. McMullen had decided to end his six month leave and announced he would be sailing in two weeks. Sturt had been detailed to the 2nd Battalion of the 5th, while he recruited for the 1st Battalion. All our talk was about the possible coming fight. Would we be there in time?

Arty and I made the round of horses, but it was really a forgone conclusion as to how we would place our money. Jannette, the 3 year old filly who had done us so well in June was being ridden by Fred Archer. Archer was undoubtedly the finest jockey England has ever produced. The combination of horse and rider was perfect. The resulting win gave the three comrades a considerable amount of money. In fact, I will say that I have never before or since had so much in winnings as we did that day.

Of course I knew that the Enderbys would be at the gathering after the races. Arty, Sutter and I were early arrivals at the festivities and, standing at the bar, began to speak of our future plans. Sutter hoped to be on his way by the end of November.

"I shall have finished this damnable course by then. Perhaps we can travel together. I'd be grateful to have an old hand with me." I told him.

"Don't see why we can't make that work" he replied "but Arty may have the war over by then and we'll miss the fun."

We laughed, but Arty's laugh was not very hearty. "It's never much fun in the Khyber Pass" he mused. "Never know which side has paid the beggars last or best, the local tribes, that is. It's all about local gain and never about the whole picture with those boys. Oh well, I'll do what I can to save you some sport." And smiling to himself, he ordered another round.

I had made a decision over the course of the summer that I needed to come on better terms with Colonel Enderby. He was now somewhat use to me and could not find an obvious reason to stifle the relationship between myself and Violet. I had also noticed the decidedly cold stares he inflicted on Lt. McMullen and Lt. Sturt but neither of them cared to offer a reason for this and I had let that issue lay.

It was the evening of the St. Leger, about midway through the evening's festivities that I found the old Colonel alone on the patio.

"Oh, Doctor Watson, come out and join me in a cigar. Beautiful night, eh? Makes one feel young and ready to retackle the world."

"Thank You, Sir. Don't mind if I do." I took the cigar proffered and lighted it. Taking a deep draught, I looked at the old man and wondered at his pleasant greeting.

"Going back soon, Sir?"

"Yes, end of the month, be back on general staff. Can't wait. Tired of all this tommy-rot sitting around. The actions in India, well some in South Africa by the looks of it, but India is the place to be."

We stood smoking for a few minutes.

"Give you a hint, Doctor. I can see you're not a mason. Oh, don't look startled, no badge or ring, you see? Lots of young men don't think about it. But if you're going to make the Army a career, you must become one. It's part of the game as they say. All my officers are masons. Look out for each other you know. Helps you make rank when you have brothers in the right places. Oh, I know it's not as important in the Medical Department. It's not like you're a line officer or something. Reason your friends McMullen and Sturt will never get anywhere. Sturt was sponsored you know, then turned it down. Said he didn't like the holier than thou attitude, ass! And

McMullen's a damned Papist. Never should have let them in the officer ranks. Oh, the Irish Catholics are alright as rankers, but they've got no place in the officer corps! And the damned impertinence of the man. Wanted to marry my daughter, can you imagine?"

I stood stunned, silent, wondering what to say, how to respond.

"Doctor," he continued, "You seem to be a good fellow. When we get to India, I'd be happy to sponsor you. Just let your commander know and we'll get it fixed up."

I had finally started to think. So this is why Arty and Sutter had made sure never to be around when Enderby was. My face started to burn and I looked at the old man in the new light of his bigotry.

"Sir, you have generously opened your home to me and for that I'm grateful." I said. "I also appreciate your advice and offer of sponsorship."

The Colonel smiled.

"But I happen to be one of those damned Papists and while I have been negligent in practicing my faith, it does preclude me from membership in an organization which hates us. As for my friends, I stand by them. Thank you for the cigar, and good night, Sir."

With this, I left the Colonel red-faced and sputtering something about ungrateful bore.

"Well you two are fine friends!" I stammered. "Let me put my foot in it with the Colonel. Why didn't you tell me?"

The two of them looked at each other and choked with laughter.

"We knew you'd get it figured out," said Sutter. "It just took you a lot longer than we thought it would."

"By God," laughed Arty. "Found out what it's like to be a "Papist", have we?"

The two of them were now slapping my back and excusing themselves from two attractive young ladies, led me to the bar.

"Three whiskies" cried Arty to the bartender.

"You should have told me! I just can't believe you didn't warn me! I thought we were friends!"

"Drink up" said Arty. "It'll all be better in the morning, and you wouldn't have believed us if we had told you, would you?"

"Well, probably not, but see here..."

"Enough" said Sutter. "You've learned a valuable lesson and we are still three comrades, with booty to split. Let's be off to London and see the town one last time before Arty sails. What about it, John?"

"Alright. But I still think you should have told me. I quite like Violet" I sulked.

Arty placed a hand on my shoulder. "Let me explain something to you, John. When you get to India you won't have a chance to worry about anything but your duties. Don't be afraid to be who you are but don't go about with a chip on your shoulder about this. The Colonel was right about one thing. Freemasons have the officer corps fairly sowed up. In fact, for a Corporal to make Sergeant means joining. Over half of the British troops in India are Catholic, most of those Irish, and yet the Army doesn't see fit to provide them a Chaplain. Only

Protestants get Chaplains. Don't get me wrong, there are some good commanders who will try to get a local padre to come by and even pay a little for them, but there are few priests. That's just how it is. Now, get your hat and we're off to London."

So, in a somewhat better mood, we three started on a new adventure.

Chapter 4

It was the 8th of October and the eve of Arty's departure. The three of us got together for dinner and a drink at Simpson's. I had spent the day at St. Bart's with some of my colleagues, going over the latest developments on the treatment of typhoid, cholera and dysentery as I knew I'd be treating more of this than I would anything else.

As we sat with our brandy at the end of the most excellent dinner, Sturt recommended that we retire to the bar at his hotel as he had some information for Arty and me.

As we sat down in the bar, Sturt called the waiter over. He arrived carrying three wooden boxes slightly larger than a cigar box.

"Thank You, Walter. Just put them down here and we'll have three whiskies if you please" said Sturt and the waiter departed.

"Here Gentleman" he continued, "is a little gift to the three of us on the eve of Arty's departure. Open your boxes please."

Inside, we each found a new Webley-Pryse, break-open revolver in .476 calibre. Each was engraved along the barrel with our names. They were fine weapons and I have used mine to good effect, I will say, ever since. These Webleys had only become available the year prior and were already quite popular because of their system for automatically ejecting the empty cartridges when they were opened. It also had a rebounding hammer. This meant that all six chambers could be loaded safely, instead of the traditional five and leaving the hammer on an empty chamber.

"I hardly know what to say!" I exclaimed.

"I hope you never have to use it John. You or Arty. But it's best to have something reliable and now you have it."

"I have more news for you, John," he went on. "Received word today that the 5th has been ordered to move from Chakrata to Afghanistan as soon as possible. Captain Beamish contacted me by wire. He's to be left at the depot with a small detachment and the women and children. He is not happy. Now, by my reckoning, there will be 27 officers, 43 sergeants, 15 drummers and roughly 690 rank and file on the march. Beamish says I'm to spend six more weeks in recruiting and then join the 5th. We'll see if we can't sail together, eh John?"

"I should enjoy that," I replied. "I'll need a hand just finding my way."

"Well here's to us and may we meet again in Kabul" said Arty, raising his glass. And so we toasted our coming adventure and the following morning Arty sailed to re-join the 18th Bombay Cavalry.

Time now started to move swiftly. I continued my studies now in earnest. The full realization that men's lives would be in my hands finally set in. I saw little of Sturt but when I did, he was always full of information. On November 7th, the 5th reached Lawrencepore and by the 20th, they were part of the Peshawar Valley Field Force assigned convoy duty for supplies going through Jamrud. On that same day, Sher Ali refused to allow the British Delegation entry into Afghanistan. The following day, the actual shooting war began as on the 21st our forces started the march for Kabul.

The 21st of November was also the eve of Sturt and I sailing to join the 5th Fusiliers. We met about nine that evening and having dispatched all but a light case to the docks, sat in the hotel bar until midnight. Sturt spent the time regaling me with stories of his family and India and he fretted about possibly missing "all the action".

As last call was sounded, we headed for the docks, Sturt had arranged an early boarding for us. We had been extremely fortunate and had gained passage on the P&O's newest liner, The Kaisar-I-Hind, which had just been christened in June. Loosely translated, it means Empress of India. She was a beautiful boat, not as fast as the trans-Atlantic kind but broader in the beam and extremely well appointed. She sported the P&O black hull, funnels and buff decks.

We sailed early on the 22nd, the same day that Lt. Gen. Sam Browne took Ali Masjid. The British field forces were losing no time on their push into Afghanistan. Sturt and I had a pleasant time and I discovered a secret known already to the regular travellers of the P&O. The secret was called the "fishing fleet". The "fishing fleet" was made up of young ladies who were looking for husbands among the outward bound diplomats, soldiers, merchants, etc. headed for India. Should they find no likely candidates, they would make the return journey on what the crew called "returned empties". I will say that Sturt and I made the acquaintance of more than one such lovely on our trip. But it was the last evening of our voyage that was to prove the most memorable for me.

We had forgone our usual evening entertaining the ladies and adjourned to the smoking room. Sturt was quite in his cups by now and as it was very late, we were alone.

"Never did tell you why that old goat Enderby doesn't like me, have I, Watson."

"No, not that it matters but I thought it was your refusal to be a mason."

Leaning across the table, he looked about the room and in a stage whisper said, "It's the treasure, you know." And smiling at his own cleverness, leaned back in his chair and took another drink.

"What treasure?"

"The one that Enderby is after and can't have," he laughed. "One more drink, old man."

Drinks came and pulling me by the sleeve he moved me to a far corner of the deserted room.

"It's like this, old family story. Seems to be true but I can't prove it yet. Enderby wants the map, you see?"

"No, I'm afraid I don't." I replied.

"How should I tell this? How familiar are you with the last Afghan war? Well, never mind, I'm sure you know about the retreat from Kabul. In the fall of '42, the East India Company was tired of paying to keep troops in Afghanistan. The company man in Kabul was named Macnaghton, real skin flint, tried to make a name for himself by declaring Kabul tamed and cutting expenses. The Major General commanding the Army forces was named Elphinstone. Old man, fought at Waterloo.

33

Elphinstone tried to get the Army in order and build a proper fort but Macnaghton was against spending the money. Macnaghton also cut in half the payments the company made that went to the tribes controlling the Khyber Pass. The tribes started raiding the convoys again and Macnaghton decided to teach them a lesson. He sent the 1st Brigade under Sir Robert Sale back to India, having them punish the Ghilzais on the way. Macnaghton thought he'd save some money and show the company how secure Kabul was. But once the first Brigade left on the 10th of October 1841, they found they had to fight their way through the Khurd-Kabul pass and had to hold up at Jalalabad.

"On the second of November, the British diplomatic representative, Sir Alexander Burnes, his brother and another officer were murdered and their compound set on fire. Soon the whole garrison was surrounded and cut off from their supplies which were a quarter mile outside their lines. There were several little forays out to drive off the Afghans but to no effect.

"Sales at the time was in Gandamak, five days away and unable to return because of the thousands of Ghilzais in between. Another column was at Kandahar 300 miles away and a relief expedition, if they could get through the passes, would be five weeks coming.

"By the 11th o f December, Macnaghton's position was hopeless, with two days of rations remaining, he negotiated with the forces of Akbar Khan. The deal was the British leave Afghanistan forever and in exchange Macnaghton was to get safe passage to India and rations. They were to leave on the 15th, but Macnaghton was too clever for himself. He stalled while trying to get the different Afghan groups to work against each other, hopefully to his advantage. Akbar was not to be toyed with and on a meeting on the 23rd of December, Macnaghton was murdered and all deals were off.

"On Christmas Day, Akbar offered to let Elphinstone take out the garrison with safe conduct if he left behind almost all his artillery, the military treasury and all families. Elphinstone knew he'd have to fight his way out, so on 6 January, 1842, Elphinstone moved out. He abandoned the sick and wounded and with 690 British soldiers, 3,800 native soldiers, 36 British women and children and 12,000 camp followers, he started for India.

"The fighting started from the first. They fought not only hostile Ghilzais, but sub-zero temperatures and snow. By the 10th, there were only 240 Europeans, a handful of sepoys and 3,000 camp followers. On the 11th, Akbar invited Elphinstone to discuss how to enforce a safe passage. Instead, he took the General prisoner. On the 13th, the last 20 men of the 44th, the final survivors, made a stand near Gandamak, where they fought with sword and bayonet, until overwhelmed. The one survivor of the march was a Dr Boydon, a regimental surgeon, who alone, made it to Jalalabad.

"Now, here's the part you don't know. On the 8th, LT Sturt, my great uncle, was killed during one of these skirmishes and on the 9th, his wife and son, along with Lady Sale and a number of others, including Elphinstone, became prisoners of Akbar.

Before he died of his wounds, LT Sturt gave his wife a map that he had been given by a friendly Afghan a few months before the siege. While the map was of the area near Jamrud, all of its inscriptions were in Latin and Greek. It meant nothing to the Afghan merchant, but LT Sturt recognized it for what it was, a map drawn by a Jesuit Monk named Benedict Goes.

"Benedict had been a Portuguese soldier in the 16th century," continued my friend. "In 1584, he became a brother of the Jesuit order in India. At the request of the Emperor Akbar in 1595 he and two others travelled to Lahore where they became fluent in Persian and learned the ways of the Saracen.

"In late 1602, he was selected to make an overland trip from India to China, at the time, no one was sure if Cathay and China were in the same place and Benedict was chosen to find out. Another Jesuit had been progressing from the China coast toward Peking, but it would take 15 years for Matteo Ricci to be allowed to reach there in 1598.

"With the blessings and financial support of Akbar, Benedict started his journey disguised as an Armenian merchant. He went from Agra to Lahore and the on to Kabul with a priest and a Greek merchant named Demetrios. The priest stayed in Kabul as did Demetrios. Benedict, calling himself Abdullah, hired a real Armenian merchant in Lahore named Isaac. Isaac would stay with Benedict all the way to China.

"While in Kabul Benedict met a lady named "Agahanem". Her brother was the ruler of Kashgaria and her son the ruler of Hotan. On her way back from a pilgrimage to Mecca, she ran out of money. Benedict befriended her and supplied the funds for her to return to her homeland. Benedict and Isaac travelled through the Hindu Kush and Northern Afghanistan and by November of 1603, they had reached Yarkand where Demetrios caught up with them. Here they stayed for a year, gathering jade for the great caravan to Cathay.

"During this time, Benedict travelled to Hotan where the Queen Mother repaid him many times over, both in jade and precious gems. Now Benedict made a decision of great consequence. He needed the jade for his impersonation to proceed, but the casket of rubies and diamond he did not want to risk on the trip. The treasure would do wonders for the Jesuit teaching mission and should be returned.

"Demetrios was assigned to start the journey back to Agra. So they parted, Demetrios to return to India and Benedict and Isaac on to Cathay. Benedict made it to China, but never to Peking, dying in Suzhou while waiting permission to continue. Isaac made it all the way to Peking, having been rescued by another Jesuit Brother, Giovanni Fernandes and taken to Ricci. Isaac returned to India by sea, but nothing more was ever seen of Demetrios. Until LT. Sturt received that map, it was thought that Demetrios had either absconded with the treasure or was killed along the way. He was killed, by Ghilzais, but not before he hid the treasure. It's this map that Enderby wants and he's not sure that I have."

"What an astounding tale," I said. "And you have this map?"

"Yes," he smiled and sat back in the chair.

"You've never actually looked for the treasure?"

"No. Never had a real chance but with the 5th moving up to Jamrud, I expect to get it."

"Best of luck," I laughed. "I expect it's long gone. Taken by the same Ghilzais who killed Demetrios and took the map."

"Think that if you want, as for me, I intend to find it."

With that, we were off to bed for a few hours sleep before arriving in Bombay. I had no idea that the treasure would overshadow my whole life.

Chapter 5

Bombay was an amazing place. The sights, sounds, even the smells were something I had never experienced. And how fortunate I was, for not only did I have Sturt, I was met by the man who would later save my life, Private Liam Murray.

Murray was about 5'10, slender, with red hair, sunburned skin, piercing blue eyes and a military moustache. "Private Murray, Sir. Been sent to help you get to the regiment. I have arranged for quarters for you until the coastal steamer leaves on Monday, and General Watson asked if you would join him tonight at his quarters. He's leaving in the morning."

So it was, that with the able assistance of Private Murray, Sturt and I dropped our kit at our quarters and went to meet my father's cousin. He's a magnificent fellow. He was in his fifties then and a more active man you never met.

Cousin John was staying at, of all places, the Watson Hotel. A magnificent 5 story hotel with an atrium and ballroom, the finest service by English waitresses and an excellent bar. The finest hotel in Bombay, it was built in England of cast iron and shipped to India one piece at a time. Murray left us to our own devices on the steps of the Watson, saying he would collect us on the morrow to see to improvements to our kit. With that, he was off, to a native pub, I imagine.

Cousin John was most amiable, asking questions of father and my brother and treating us to dinner and drinks. It was after dinner that he called one of the waitresses over.

"Sally, bring out that box I left with you, eh girl?"

Going to the pantry, she returned in a moment.

"Here you are, Sir."

"Good Girl, now bring another round, will you?"

"Here my boy is a little something for you. All the officers are having them made. Very helpful on campaign, called a Browne Belt. Old Sam Brown developed it, much better than issue equipment. Lost his left arm you see in the mutiny. Sabre kept banging around so he came up with this system, quite a good show.

"I see the 5th is up on the Khyber, you should see some action, but I hope you aren't kept too busy doctor." He smiled.

"Tell me, Sir. How bad is it in Afghanistan?" I asked.

"Oh, we'll pull through to Kabul. Their problem is the tribes can never unify. Each will change sides depending on the last battle. Remember that. None of these Afghans are to be trusted."

And with that small bit of advice, the evening closed. Cousin John was off in the morning and Sturt and I were back to our hotel and for two busy days occupied our time seeing what we could of Bombay and collecting additional equipment.

On the morning following my meeting with Cousin John, I discovered that Murray had taken my whites to be dyed khaki by a local merchant with the promise of a return in time for our sailing on the 9th.

So three days after arriving in Bombay, Sturt, Murray and I sailed on the British India steamer, Vingorla, for Karachi. It was a three day trip at about 8 knots. The Vingorla carried salon passengers and cargo along with deck passengers. She relied on steam and sail and her captain JW Stuart was a young man who ran a taught ship.

While sitting in the salon on the second night, Sturt talked to me about his revelation of the treasure. As we sat smoking our cigars, I asked where his ancestor had actually come upon the map he now held.

"You may know that there is a small Armenian Catholic community in Afghanistan. In both Lahore and in Kabul, they have their own churches. The Jesuits in India had been in touch with them even in the time of Benedict, although they came under the authority of the Armenian Apostolic Church in Esfahan. They were mostly merchants but in Lahore they were fine gun makers. In 1755, the gun makers were forcibly moved from Lahore to Kabul and it is thought the map, along with their other church treasures, came with them. About 1830 these people were abandoned by the Armenian Church and no more priests were sent. The Armenians did the best they could, but many of their books and documents could not be read as they only spoke Persian and possessed papers in Greek and Latin as well.

"My ancestor became friendly with these folks in Kabul, many times visiting their church which sits in the shadow of Fort Bala Hissan. It was during one of these visits to the Church that he discovered the map. At first, he thought it only an interesting map of

41

the Khyber area, and he was given the map by the Armenian elder as a gift for his kindness to them and interest in their community. They, of course, unable to read it, had no idea what it represented. And it was only after some months that LT. Sturt was able to piece together its meaning. It was shortly after this that he met his end in the retreat. He never had a chance to look for the treasure.

"Amazing" I said. "And will you really look for it?"

"No, Watson. We will look for it! I don't suppose this is a one man job and I can't think of a better partner. What do you say, are you in for an adventure? I've already talked to Arty."

"Of course," I replied, "but where will we find the time? What with the campaign and all, we've no chance."

"Oh, we'll make short work of these Afghans, I've no doubt of that and then we'll have all the time in the world."

So we left it. We were now both Army officers and treasure hunters. First to fight the war and then to find the treasure, what excitement.

We arrived in Karachi the afternoon of 11 December, and disembarked. It was a short wait of only three days in Karachi as there were supply trains leaving almost daily to the north. It was here we met Mr Frederick Dibble, a civil engineer with the railroad who was returning from leave.

Having rested and gathered our kit, Sturt, Murray and I boarded the train that would take us north to Lahore. The train was a sight to behold, pulled by an engine that probably saw it's best days twenty years prior and made up of three coaches and a half dozen freight cars. Sturt, Murray, Dibble and I shared two bench seats in the first car. Every inch of every car was filled with all forms of freight and humanity. Soldiers, merchants, paupers, men, women and children rode in and on the cars as we pulled out of Karachi.

"You Gentlemen are quite fortunate," said Dibble. "We have made great progress on the railroad in the last few months. We will be in Lahore in less than 48 hours where we will rid ourselves of all the natives. From there to Jhelum, the railroad has been commandeered by the Army. It's the railhead at the moment but we're pushing on steadily. Tough going because of the mountains. We hope to be in Peshawar in two years. That is if you boys can keep the natives under control."

"We're going on to Jamrud. How do we continue?" I asked.

"Well, by foot, I'm afraid. It's about 180 miles to Peshawar but the military road is very good. Is that where you're headed?"

"Yes, I'm afraid," Said Sturt. "Gets kind of tough from Peshawar."

"Yes, I suppose, but only 8 miles. Your first stop will be Rawal Pindi. It's about 68 miles. You'll get a break there. The horse carts are a little rough on the nerves. We have to change trains twice before we even get to Lahore. There are still no bridges over the Sutlej at Adamwahan or the Indus at Sukkur, but we're working on it."

So we passed the next 48 hours by rail and ferry and arriving at Lahore, connected with a troop train for Jhelum. Another day saw us at the great supply depot. Here we were met by LT Thomas Godard of the 5th who had been sent to gather supplies, recruits and horses. It was here my official duties began as I attempted to assemble three horse carts filled with medical supplies from a list supplied by Lt. Godard in response to a request of the Principle Medical Officer (PMO) Dr James Hanbury. With Murray's help and Godard's firm hand, we filled the carts.

We left Jhelum on the 20th, an amazing caravan which included horse carts and camels, foot soldiers and cavalry and a vast assortment of camp followers trying to sell their wares. At the end of the first day, we had made 20 miles. Godard, Sturt and I had been well mounted on native ponies and so the next morning we decided to push on to Rawal Pindi and let the caravans catch up the following day. The medical supplies were left in Murray's capable hands. We arrived at Rawal Pindi to find news that General Browne had taken Jalalabad. True soldiers that they were, Godard and Sturt were both joyous at the news and disappointed not to be in the fight.

"Damn thing will be over before we're in it," complained Godard.

"Lots more to do before we get to Kabul," responded Sturt, "but I don't want to waste time here. Suppose we press on in the morning for Peshawar? We can make it in three days even with the climb."

To this proposal, I resisted. I reminded Godard of his duty to get the 5th supplies forward, and I had no desire to abandon Murray and the medical kits.

Late the next afternoon, the caravans arrived. Godard had made arrangements to secure the 5th's supply carts and I had spent the day in the local infirmary assisting on cases. Most of which were minor.

Early on the 23rd, we pushed on with the caravan toward Peshawar. Somewhere on the road, we celebrated Christmas 1878 and arrived in Peshawar late on the 27th. The following morning we joined the regiment at Jamrud.

Chapter 6

Our commander was Lieutenant Colonel Rowland. Fine fellow, well bred, who cared greatly for his men. He was the kind of commander who led soldiers, not ordered them into battle without sharing their trials. On the day we met, he had been recently back from an excursion in the Bazar Valley with 300 men. They had met little opposition.

Sturt had taken me to the headquarters directly on arriving in Jamrud and we were passed directly in to see the colonel.

"Lieutenant Sturt, reporting, Sir. Lieutenant Godard is seeing to the delivery of supplies to Commissary O'Rourke and will be along directly. And this is Assistant Surgeon, John Watson, been assigned to us, Sir."

"Good to see you Sturt. We've been a little short on duty officers. Glad to have you back," said Rowland with a smile. "and Dr Watson. I understand you have significant qualifications as a surgeon. I hope we never have need of you, unfortunately, we probably will. Murray taking good care of you?"

"Excellent care, Sir. May I say that I too hope you don't need my skills."

We all laughed and I knew this was a commander one could rely on. He would not just accomplish a mission, he would also see to the needs of his soldiers.

"Well, Doctor," he continued, "We'll let Murray see you over to the infirmary; the Surgeon-Major should be over there. As you know, surgeons and commissary officers are not normally members of the mess, but I think we're all in this together so in the 1st battalion, you're our permanent guest. We'll see you this evening. Murray," he called, "Show Dr Watson to the infirmary, will you? And Sturt, you stay here. I've some things to catch you up on. 'Till tonight, Doctor." With that, I was dismissed and Murray and I went to the infirmary.

The infirmary was fairly small, 12 or 15 beds. Murray introduced me to Surgeon-Major Thomas Bennet. Bennet, I knew, had been in the Army since the mutiny and had served in posts across the world. My first impression was a little disappointing. He was short, probably 5'6" and heavy set with drooping eyes and the nose of a drinker. He looked older than his 50 odd years, but his smile was bright and genuine and I could see the orderlies thought the world of him.

"Come in. Come in Doctor," he called cheerily from a tiny closet of an office. "Glad to have you, young man. Always need help we'll have you know. Understand you've had an uneventful trip, most unusual in India to have uneventful trips. But come in, sit down and tell me about your journey."

I thanked him for his welcome and detailed my qualifications to him, which he seemed to take in with interest.

"Horseman?" he asked.

"I like to think I am."

"Good. Good, that will be helpful. Can't ride well myself anymore. Still limp from 20 years ago, stiff leg won't sit in the saddle long and we need to send someone along on some of these little forays they like to go on. Let me see, what do I need to tell you?

"Let's start with the hospital here. Just 15 beds, mostly sickness right now. Large hospital in Peshawar, 50 beds moving up to Jalalabad. Right now we are well off on supplies but our problem is people. We are understrength in orderlies, have no hospital sergeant or writer and the doolie bearers aren't much use. We just have to make do and hope for the best. Let's see. What else can I tell you?"

"What is the 5th supposed to be doing?" I asked.

"Ah, well, that's pretty simple. They provide two things. Escort of convoys between Peshawar and Jalalabad and go on little excursions around the area to punish the tribes that don't stay in line. Keeps the poor fellows moving about all the time. Still, that's better than just sitting. Less likely to malinger if they have something to do, you know. And now that the Amir has fled Kabul, with the Russians we won't be here long."

"The Amir has left?"

"Yes, yes, left his son Sadar Yakub Khan in Kabul, as I say, maybe we can make an end of this and get back. But now, let me show you around and you can get settled in."

So I started my official duties with the 5th. The next few weeks were dull indeed. Little happened at our infirmary except the constant coming and going of soldiers with the usual blisters and boils, cuts and scrapes and an occasional fever. It seems that the 5th's long time in India had indeed toughened the men, most of whom were the old 21 year enlistments.

During those weeks it was not unusual for Sutter to come visit me or I him. The boredom of convoy escort was starting to show and Sutter had once again turned his attention to the Jesuit treasure. As we sat one night in my quarters with a bottle of whiskey he took out the map and placed it on the table.

"John, the best I can tell, this village here is Kam Dakka," he said, pointing to the centre of the map. "Now look to the northeast here. It appears to be a trail leading what must be 10 or 12 miles to the base of these foothills and then to a valley, all of which is filled by bloody tribesmen. And here," stabbing with his finger, "are the words 'Confianca Sagzado', which is Portuguese for "Sacred Trust'. That must be where the treasure is."

I took out my ordnance map of the area and laid it beside the treasure map and we spent the next while comparing villages and mountain tops.

"It certainly seems to be Kam Dakkar, I must admit but it's the trail that doesn't seem right. Our map doesn't show it at all after about a mile."

"Probably couldn't take the time to survey in that direction," sighed Sutter. "We'll have to find time to scout out that way if we can ever break free of this damned convoy duty."

"Something else is odd about this map of yours."

"What would that be?"

"In the four corners are crosses, quite understandable, but three are Roman crosses and the fourth is Eastern Orthodox. Curious."

"Well, the Jesuits were Roman Church and I suppose he added the fourth in deference to the Armenians."

"Possible," I replied. "What was that noise?"

"Hello chaps" came a voice as I turned toward the door. It was Godard. "Having a conference?"

"Just looking over some maps of the area, need to know your surroundings," replied Sutter, gathering up his map as I started folding mine.

"Excellent. Just came to get you Sturt. Colonel needs you. We're to go up the Bazar again. You too, Doctor. One ambulance wagon, you and a couple orderlies, and whoever you need in Doolie bearers. Best get the word out. Later." And with that, he turned and was gone.

"How long do you thing he was listening, John?"

"Surely not, he just came with the orders."

"Maybe," he said slowly. "Maybe. Well, off to the old man. Best get your kit."

It was a hurried night. My first experience of a military expedition. It seemed that Major Cavagnari, the political officer, felt that good results could be made of a show of force in the valley. The Jamrud column, of which we were a part, was only one of three converging on the valley.

What an amazing sight it was. Over 1200 soldiers in a single column. Elephants loaded with artillery, the 5th Fusiliers, the 25th foot, native lancers and infantry and an assortment of bhisti's and doolie bearers and the like.

We left Jamrud early on the 24th. I still had my fine native horse(whom I had named Emmett) and Murray drove a four mule team from the ambulance box. We had one other orderly and four bearers.

The dust was the worst of it. The slow moving column must have been visible for miles by the dust cloud, and at the end of the day it lay heavy on and in everything. As we camped for the night, cook fires were lighted and picquets were sent out. All through that first night, and during the entire rest of the expedition, you could hear the picquets exchanging fire with the Afghans. Fortunately, the first few nights saw no work for my little section.

On the 26th of January, we met with a column from Ali Masjid, adding another 1200 soldiers. On the next day, in the Bazar Valley Plain, we camped with yet another thousand men from the Basawal Column. That night Sutter found time to stop by for a pipe. By now, I was treating cuts and bangs and blisters but nothing of significance, so we had time to sit and contemplate the massive force camped before us.

"When you look at a sight like this, you can't contemplate failure, can you?" mused Sutter.

"No, I suppose not. But what a queer question?"

"Oh, we'll win this little war, no doubt, but in the long run, I think the natives will have it all their own way. We can't stay here forever and once we're gone, well, it's back to the usual for them. Anyway, still no time for our little adventure, eh?"

"No," I replied. "But we'll get there."

For a long time that night we just sat and smoked. The next few days were filled with movement. The Zakha Khal Afridis were definitely hostile. We were fired on constantly from the hillsides but never would they come forward for a fight. They also burned their own villages prior to our arrival. It was a bad sight as we had received direct orders not to molest any of the villages. By the 3rd of February, we were on our return to Jamrud having punished the Afridis at a cost of about a dozen wounded to us. So ended my first experience on the active march.

The next few weeks were the usual dull routine. That is, until the visit of the Commander In Chief for India, Sir F.P. Haines. We had but a day's notice of his visit which would include a parade of the entire 2nd Division and an inspection of our medical facility. His trip onward from Jamrud as far as the Shahqai was protected by the 5th with a soldier on every hill.

Sir Haines' visit to our hospital was memorable in several ways. Firstly, he was well pleased with our facility, but it was who came with him, who would impact me more. As I stood awaiting Sir Haines' arrival, in walked Colonel Enderby. He appeared not surprised at all, and to his side, walked Lt. Godard.

"I see you've made yourself at home, Doctor." Smiled the Colonel. A smile of pure malevolence. "Hope you enjoy these backwaters, Watson. Could have gotten you on staff you know. Need to be more prudent how you pick your battles. Well, seen all I need to Godard. Let's move on. Good Day, Doctor."

My mouth was open as they left. But that wasn't my only surprise. LT McMullen appeared the moment they left.

"Don't let the old bastard get to you, John. He's as big an ass as ever. Doesn't mind sending other people on forlorn hopes! Well close your mouth and offer me some medicinal brandy, eh?"

"Arthur, good fellow, of course, of course! What are you doing here?"

"Oh, escort with the Commander. We've a squadron of the 18th at Peshawar and I've got a detachment with me. All pomp and show, you know. Have a detachment from nearly every cavalry and lancer regiment around traveling with the entourage. So, how have you been?"

We spent the next few moments in pleasant conversation when Arty had to leave for Ali Masjid with his detail. It was good to know there was another friend in the area.

That night Sutter and I met as usual at the mess and taking a small corner table, started discussing the surprises of the day.

"Not a shot fired from Jamrud to Ali Masjid today. They say Sir Haines was impressed. That's good, I suppose. Saw Arty, said he talked with you at the hospital, but he wanted to pass something on to us. He said, watch out for Godard. Evidently, Godard has been down to see Enderby on at least two occasions. They're way too chummy. Arty just has a feeling about things."

"Have you been able to do any scouting?" I asked.

"Not much, being so far off the road, it's not really in our bailiwick. Hard to justify the risk. Been about 3 miles along the trail. It's definitely there beyond what the survey crew put down. We'll get a chance at it, I'm sure."

It would take another two months but circumstances would lead us to Dakka and give us a chance to continue the search.

As the warmer weather of March started, so sickness began to take its toll. The constant convoy duty and work parties were starting to wear on the men of the 5th. It was now not uncommon to have 10 to 15 in hospital at one time. Cholera would be our constant companion. Even with my special knowledge, many would not be saved and it has always worn on me. Somehow, I should have saved them. In all that year, we lost 2 sergeants and 35 rank and file, heart-breaking.

Around about the 1st of March, we got the news of Sher Ali's death the month prior. Surely we could negotiate with his successor Yakub Khan. Of course, as it turned out, we could not. The fighting would continue, and soon.

Chapter 7

I sat writing reports on the afternoon of the 23rd when Murray came in with word to pack up the ambulance wagon and be ready to march that night. I left Murray and the doolie bearers to get our equipment ready and went in search of information.

At the headquarters, I found Surgeon-Major Bennett in conference with Major Tucker, our second in command.

"Watson," cried Bennett. "Over here. Seems you're going to a little tussle down the road. Nothing you can't handle. The Major here assures me you'll be back in a couple of days. Don't enjoy yourself too much." Bennett smiled and Tucker looked irritated. I knew there was something else and on Bennett's leaving for the mess and another whiskey, Tucker took me over to the wall map.

"Look here, Doctor," he said pointing to a point to our west. "This is where you're going. Deh-Sarakh is a plains area near our fort in Pesh-Bolak. Seems a Jemadar was leading a foraging part out there when he was jumped by about 300 Afridis. He did a fine job though, camels to the rear, retired in good order to Pesh-Bolak. Now the political officers say we need to go punish the natives. Sir Sam Browne is sending a force under BG Tyler to punish the blighters. The 5th has been tasked for 150 bayonets. You're going along to patch the boys up. Don't suspect it'll amount to much though. Better you than that drunk you call Surgeon-Major! Anyway, be ready by midnight."

With that bit of information, I was off to see that Murray had the requisite supplies, when I was stopped by a call from behind.

"Dr Watson!" came the shout.

Turning, I found Sutter trotting toward me on his bay. Before he even reached me, he had leaped from his horse and ran toward me. Throwing his arm around my shoulder, he whispered in my ear, "I found it! By God, I found it!" He was shaking with excitement.

"The treasure?" I blurted out.

"Quiet, quiet," he admonished. "Well no, but a Roman cross about 3 ½ miles up the trail. Plain as day, chiselled on a rock on the side of the trail, it must mean I'm on the right track. It must! Grab your kit and we'll go back and look."

"But I can't," I moaned. "We're off on an expedition tonight. I can't leave."

The disappointment showed in his face.

"Lt. Sturt," came a voice, it was Sgt Ryan. "The Colonel is looking for you. Moving out tonight, Sir. You're to report immediately."

"Damn and bother! Alright, Sergeant, on the way. Doctor, not a word."

"Sutter, you know I won't," I complained.

"I know, must report. See you later." And with that, he was off to headquarters.

The next I saw Sturt was about one in the morning as the column started for the Deh-Sarakh plains. It was a fairly formidable force, or so I thought, of 500 bayonets, 150 lances and two cannons.

As we moved toward Pesh-Bolak in the darkness, our little ambulance choked on the dust of the column. Being mounted, I was able to, now and then, move to the upwind side of the column and avoid some of the dust. I also took the privilege of moving up the column to ride with Sturt at the head of his two companies from the 5th.

"You know, Sutter, just a cross on a rock doesn't mean you're on the right track," I said, riding up alongside him.

"John, it must!" he looked around to see that no one was close. "I have it figured out now that I've seen the cross. Remember the four corners of the map? Those Roman crosses and a Byzantine. It must mean follow those three to the one!" His face was flush with excitement.

"Yes, well, it's possible," I contemplated. "But that's an awful long stretch. That one cross may mean nothing. Quiet! Godard!"

I had noticed Godard coming up on our left out of the corner of my eye.

"Conspiring, are we?" he smirked.

"Sturt was just explaining our mission. Quite interesting. Hope the politicos are right and there won't be much action."

"Can't get promoted if there isn't any action, eh Sturt?"

"Can't take casualties if the enemy doesn't fight and that's fine with me," replied Sturt. "Best get back to your company, Godard, I can see Pesh-Bolak up in the distance." With that, Godard reigned up and turned back.

"Best do the same, John. Sun's coming up and we'll get busy. And trust no one!" he called as I turned my horse back to the ambulance.

As I turned, I could see the 11th and 13th Bengal Lancers picking up the pace and leaving the infantry and guns behind. No matter Sturt's wishes, it looked like there would be action.

We continued past Pesh-Bolak and by mid morning were into the Deh-Sarakh Plain. I was riding alongside the ambulance when Murray suddenly stood, reigns in hand, squinting into the distance.

"What is it?"

"I can hear rifle fire, Sir. It's up ahead to the south."

I now realized that besides the creaking harness and the grinding of the iron tires, there was indeed the distant pop of carbines and muskets. The column had also sprung to life. The infantry was suddenly moving at the double quick and the artillery had moved to the left of the column and was sprinting ahead.

"Stay with the 5th!" I called to Murray and spurring my horse, rode for the front. I crested a large hill the same time as the infantry and came upon B.G. Tyler and his staff. To their front, dismounted lancers were returning fire to both a small village to our left and to the fort of Mausam about 750 yards to our front.

Sturt arrived just then with his two companies of the 5th, along with a lieutenant from the 17th Foot who also had two companies. B.G. Tyler ordered the 5th to relieve the 13th Lancers who were fighting on foot, the 17th and the two half companies of Indian troops stood in reserve.

The fortified village stood on high ground of Safed Koh. To our right was a deep nala or drainage ditch and on the left, another. The walls of the fort and the towers were filled with Shinwaris. They had also poured out of the gate and filled the nala. Even I could tell we were greatly outnumbered.

The guns of the Royal Artillery were being unlimbered as the 11th Bengal Lancers returned from an abortive attack on the east nala. I watched the 13th remount and fall back, replaced by the men of the 5th. The 13th rode out of sight to the southwest.

The Royal Artillery guns opened fire on Mausam. Their fire was both accurate and devastating. Round after round crashed into the fort and the tower, tearing gaping holes in the walls and sending bodies to be buried under the rubble. But most impressive of all were the artillerymen themselves. Rifle fire from the nearby village of Darwazai constantly rained upon them, striking dirt and boxes and occasionally an animal or piece of equipment, yet the gunners calmly went about their duties. Their officers stood in full view, giving corrections for the firing of each shell. Truly a wonder to watch.

Murray had arrived with the ambulance and I instructed him to keep with me. The Shinwaris were now abandoning the fort, not able to withstand the cannon fire. The infantry, in mass, was now ordered to advance and our little ambulance followed at a distance of about 200 yards. Rifle fire now spit all around us as the few Afghans left in Mausam had their fire increased by the men in the west nala who could now fire on the infantry.

Springing from the earth behind the west nala appeared the 13th Lancers. Captain Thompson and his 60 men seized their chance. With 800 rifles concentrating on the infantry advance, he boldly ordered his men to charge. Completely surprised by the attack, the Afghans got off a single volley, unhorsing nine, but the surprise was so complete all resistance ceased and flight became the natural instinct. The Lancers pursued them into the foothills, killing 50, the Shinwaris did not stop until they were on the hills a mile distant.

As our infantry poured into Mausam there only remained a single Afghan locked in a tower, sniping as best he could and holding the entire column at bay. Anyone who showed his face was liable to be shot at. No one could get near the tower. As the rest of the infantry went about the business of destroying the other towers, Sturt tried to decide how to take this single man. He finally did it by climbing another tower and in an exchange of fire, killed the last defender.

Murray and I were exceedingly busy. While there were no casualties in the 5th, there were two dead Sowars and a dozen wounded. I, being the only doctor, treated each as quickly as possible. Fortunately, all the wounded but two were fairly minor. So as the infantry set about blowing up the towers, Murray and I patched and sewed and moved on to those of our enemy too wounded to be carried away by their comrades. Here I learned another lesson of war, for as I was about to amputate a leg, the call came to form up. We were retiring and the Afghan wounded would be left to their own. I couldn't take them, the ambulance was full of dead and wounded Sowars, and I couldn't stay. I left behind at least two dozen men that I knew native medicine wouldn't save.

As our little ambulance drove past the village of Darwazai, the village that had fired on us, I saw the Indian sepoys move hut to hut, burning the village to the ground and destroying the towers.

"Sir," it was Murray. "In the road there," he pointed to what I first took for a pile of rags. "I think that woman is wounded."

I jumped down from my horse and approaching, found a young Shinwari woman. She was unconscious and having obviously been caught in the crossfire, had been wounded in the shoulder. It was not a bad wound but the shock and loss of blood had done their work.

"Hold up, Murray. Let's find some room in that wagon."

Picking her up, I placed her on the wagon and handing the reigns of my horse to a doolie bearer, climbed in.

"Keep moving," I instructed. "We can't fall behind."

The moment the columns had blown the towers and evacuated Mausam, the Shinwari had swarmed back in. They were on our heels as we left Darwazai in flames and started to fill the hillsides. By now, tribesman from the whole area were assembling, perhaps 3,000 fighters now trailed our force of 700.

As we moved along, I cut the cloth from the woman's shoulder. She was lucky; the bullet had gone all the way through, leaving a clean wound. Antiseptic and bandage was the best I could do as the spring less wagon continued to move. Leaving the wounded in the ambulance, I reclaimed my horse and went in search of Sutter, finding him on the left of the column.

"What the hell are we into?" I asked.

"We're alright," he replied. Suddenly,   the cannons cracked and shell landed just 500 yards to our rear, scattering a large group of Shinwaris.

Coming back up from a crouch, I called to Sturt, "You're sure?"

"Yes" He laughed. "We've got Lancers caring for the flanks and we are retiring by alternating lines. The guns will help them stay back."

"Hope you're right!"

"I am, not to worry. And by the way," he said looking around, "don't flinch in front of the men. Bad form, old boy, gets them concerned."

So we continued for the next ten miles. There were 3,000 tribesmen ebbing and flowing against our flanks and rear, sometimes coming within 100 yards of our line. It was not until we reached the walls of Pesh-Bolak that they retired. We heard the next day that they had lost 160 dead and 300 wounded. But I again had learned a valuable lesson. Had the Shinwaris been well armed instead of using 300 year old matchlocks, or had the different villages and tribes been able to coordinate and form a coherent command, our little expedition would not have ended so well.

Chapter 8

It was at Pesh-Bolak that I made the decision that I must find a way to provide medical treatment to the Afghans. Following a day of rest under the walls of the fort, I saw amazing improvement in my native patient, but I could not get her to speak. As I cleaned her wound, she would only stare in another direction, never looking at me or answering the smiles with which I tried to reassure her.

My first problem was that as a woman, she had to be kept segregated from the sowars. None of them would remain in the same room with her and would rather forego treatment than have their bodies exposed in any way to her.

My second problem was the language barrier. She spoke only Dari. I, of course, had picked up a few phrases, but nothing useful in such a situation. Fortunately there was a native orderly named Guhkta with the 27th Punjab Infantry who was in the little infirmary who could speak her language.

Guhkta had been a hospital assistant in the Indian Army back to before the mutiny. He was a kind fellow, always a smile, nothing too hard for him to accomplish. Between he and Murray, there quickly became a bond, both professional and personal. I think that for a few months, they became like the brothers that neither had.

On the second day of our stay at Pesh-Bolak, it was Guhkta who got our little patient to speak. Her name was Malalai. She was about 19 years old. She was not a native of the Darawazai village where we found her. Only the night before our attack, she had been traded by her father for a debt owed of nine goats.

"Traded for nine goats?" I exclaimed, standing with Guhkta at her cot. "Who the devil trades people for goats?"

"You do not understand, Sahib, this is most common," said Guhkta. "Women are traded among the hill tribes all the time in payment of debts. Sometimes, if one man should kill another, he will give his daughter or sister to the other family in payment. It ties the families together, or so it is supposed. Most times it ends in the death of the girl in a short time."

Guhkta spoke to the girl again and then turned back to me.

"She wants to know if she will die. I told her no, she will live, thanks to the English Doctor."

"Yes, she'll pull through all right. We can leave her here when we return to Jamrud tomorrow."

Guhkta translated my statement to the girl. She looked at me with such a sad face. She actually was quite beautiful. About five foot tall and if she weighed 100 pounds, I'd have been surprised. Dark skin, coal black hair and eyes. The kind of eyes that spoke. She spoke to Guhkta.

"She cannot be left here Sahib, she knows no one and if you send her back, she will be stoned to death for going off with the English devils. She wants to go with you."

"Bloody hell, she can't come with us. It's a military column, tell her."

"She will not listen, Sahib, and if you leave her she will kill herself rather than be stoned."

"Damndest country I ever saw. Alright, I'll do this much. I'll keep her in the ambulance as a patient until we get to Jamrud, but then she's on her own. Make sure she understands." And with those words, I turned and left.

The following morning we left Pesh-Bolak on our way to Jamrud. The sole occupant of our little ambulance was Malalai as we left the sowars in hospital. On our short journey, I wondered how I could explain my new ward to Bennett. Morning and night, I changed her bandage and we started the game of learning to speak to each other. With the help of Guhkta, I was learning to communicate and so we pointed and spoke and smiled. I became her tutor and she mine. An attachment had begun. I went to Bennett that first day back and explained what I wanted to do, start a treatment centre for locals. To my surprise, he was very receptive to the idea.

"I've thought the same for a long time, Watson. There are three of us here and we aren't all that busy. You know, of course, that Fort Dakka has already started a clinic, regular hospital there, so they have what they need."

"Perhaps I can go see what they're doing? It would give me an idea for a starting place. We'll need supplies and native speakers and who knows what."

"I'm sure that won't be a problem. Our boys travel the road every day on convoy duty. Why don't you just go with the next convoy? I'm sure I can get it cleared with Rowland."

"Well, I do have a bit of a problem I have to take care of, if I can explain."

"Whiskey?" said Bennett, offering a glass.

"No, not before morning brunch, thanks." The frustration in my voice must have showed for he put down the glass and sat back in his chair.

"And the problem is?"

I explained how I had found Malalai at the roadside in Darawazai, treated her wounds and brought her back to Jamrud.

"Yes, I see. Is she now able to leave?"

"She will be in a day or two, but who will take care of her wounds? She needs care for a couple weeks to be sure that it heals properly."

"Like her, don't you."

"No, no, it's just a case of common decency." I blustered. "I can't save her life and turn her out to die. It would be heartless. If she'd been a dog, I'd have shot her. But she's not a dog, she's a human being. Surely we can help."

Bennett smiled and looked at his glass. I could feel the heat in my face that must have shown and realized that I did like the girl. I felt sorry for her, but I liked her too.

"Let's do this, old man. She can rest until the wounds healed. Then, if you get this clinic up and running, we'll need some females to help. You can put her to work, fair enough?"

"Quite a good idea, Sir. I'll start looking for an area in the village to put the clinic. Just outside the gate would be best."

"Go ahead and look, but we need to wait for permission. Not only Rowland, but the Fort Commander will have to approve. I'll let you know."

Here the usual bureaucracy took control. It was nearly a week before Bennett informed me of the command's conditional approval. In the meantime, I had located a building not far from the gate and near an open square. My young patient was doing well also. Each day I found myself spending more and more time with her, trying to teach the phrases I knew she would need to know. Murray and Guhkta would help me teach and Malalai was a quick learner. To tell the truth, it was good to have a project other than normal rounds.

The conditional approval came with a caveat. I must supply a requisition document which included not only number of personnel to be used in what capacity, but what stores would be used and a cost for hiring native help.

To get this kind of data, I knew I had to travel to Dakka and get the advice of those currently running the native clinic. So in late April, I went to find Sturt and ask about convoys to Dakka. I had seen little of him since I had started the new project.

Finding Sturt's quarters empty, I found his orderly who informed me that he and two sepoys from the 27th had gone on a mission to gather information on the Mohmands north of the Kabul River.

At the headquarters, Major Tucker informed me that Lt. Godard would be taking his company on convoy duty the following day to Dakka. I received permission to accompany the convoy. And so on the

19th, Murray, I and two doolie bearers found ourselves, once again at the tail end of a convoy ingesting huge quantities of dust.

Except for some intermittent and ineffective sniping from the hillsides, the company passed in relative calm. Telegraph wire had been strung the entire distance and we passed wire parties all along the way, repairing the breaks that were caused daily by the Afghans.

Arriving in Dakka late that evening, Murray saw to bedding down the mules and the bearers. I went in search of the hospital where I was well received by my fellow doctors.

Leaving a tour and discussion of the native clinic to the morrow, we retired to the mess and spent an hour or two. I'm afraid I don't recall the names of the doctors who were there. At any rate, the following day, Murray and I were treated to a tour of the hospital facility and the Afghan clinic. While I asked questions, Murray kept notes for me. The clinic was seeing upwards of 150 civilians a day now. Surely an impressive number and I only hoped our new clinic would not be quite so popular.

Our fact finding done, I found that the 5th would not be returning to Jamrud until the 23rd and so though other units would be headed back earlier, I decided to take the opportunity to spend a few days at the hospital. As it turned out, this was a most fortuitous decision.

Early the next day, I sent a wire to Jamrud asking if Sturt had returned. I had reason to be concerned. I knew that Sturt must have volunteered for his reconnaissance. It would give him the excuse he was looking for to penetrate deeper up the trail toward the treasure.

The Political Officer, Captain Trotter, had assured all that the Mohmands were not going to be a problem on the south side of the Kabul River, but the conventional thinking had been that they were massing on the north side for a foray. It was this information that Sturt had been sent to assess.

My concern had been raised that morning by Colonel Barnes' decision to take two guns of the Royal Artillery, a squadron of his own 10th Bengal Lancers and 3 companies of the Mhairwara Infantry on a reconnaissance in force toward Kam Dakka, about 7 miles distant, down by the Kabul River. Such a forcible recon meant Barnes was concerned about the Mohmands.

A reply to my wire came stating that Sturt had not returned and that he was twelve hours overdue. I went to find Godard.

"Nothing we can do, old man. We have our orders and besides, where would I look for him? If the Colonel wants to send us looking for him, fine. But you and I both know that won't happen. Too early any way. He'll show up, rest assured." And with those words, Godard dismissed the thought of looking for my friend. He was right, of course. Three men stood a far better chance of going unseen and surviving than a whole company. The company would have been swallowed up and annihilated by thousands of tribesmen.

About three in the afternoon, my concerns were somewhat relieved with the return of COLONEL Barnes. Having left his guns and cavalry after only 4 miles, he had gone on to Kam Dakka with his infantry. The guns were left behind because they were unable to traverse the goat trail that led through the hills of Kam Dakka Pass. The cavalry was left to support the guns as it was hard going for anything but infantry.

Arriving at Kam Dakka, a village that had proffered loyalty to the Crown, Barnes was welcomed by the village elders and asked by them to stay and help provide protection for the village. Unable to stay, Barnes returned to Dakka, but with the feeling of having abandoned his allies. That afternoon Barnes put together a mule train back at Dakka and by 5 o'clock, Capt. Creagh of the 10th Mhairwara was leading a column of 2 companies with extra ammunition, rations and entrenching tools back to Kam Dakka. COLONEL Barnes was fairly confident there would be little trouble but did not like the thought of leaving a friendly village unprotected. During the whole day's march, he had only been fired on a few times and then only from the north side of the river.

There was still no word from Sutter. Later that night, as Murray and I stood and talked outside the hospital, we watched a Jemadar and his platoon escorting a number of mules loaded with more ammunition boxes start toward Kam Dakka.

"You can never have enough ammunition, Sir," said Murray. "At least all those fellows use the same type."

"The same type?" I asked.

"Yes, all those short rifles they carry use .577 ammo. Our boys have Martinis. Different ammo. Can't share in a pinch, you see?"

"Hadn't really thought about it. It should all be the same, shouldn't it?" I mused.

"It's all left over from the mutiny, Sir. Always keep the native troops one piece of equipment behind. Keep the edge. Just in case, you see?"

"Yes, always that lurking fear, eh?"

"Yes, Sir. It's why the native artillery doesn't get anything but the little mountain cannon. Royal Artillery and Royal Horse keep the big stuff. We're all on the same side though, maybe!" Murray chuckled. "Night, Sir. See you in the morning."

Murray had given me much to think about that night.

We were at breakfast the following morning when a message arrived from Creagh for Colonel Barnes. Turning to the Political Officer, Barnes asked, "What the hell is going on with your tribesmen, Trotter?"

"Sir?"

"Message from Creagh. 'Elders refuse us entry into Kam Dakka Village. Want us to leave as we have no cannon. Have set up defensive position. Send instructions.' Well what now?"

"I don't understand, Sir. Perhaps if I went there and talked to the elders myself."

"Right, see the Major for an escort and tell Creagh to bring those two companies back if they don't want help."

Godard leaned over the table toward me. "That's the hell of this country. People always changing sides, never know who your friends are," he whispered.

The way Godard looked at me, I wasn't sure if he was talking about the natives or using it as a chance to suggest something else.

"Some of us know who our friends are," I replied.

Godard looked steadily at me. "I wonder, old boy. I wonder."

It was about an hour and half later that I saw a scramble going on in Godard's company. Water bottles being filled, packs strapped, weapons checked.

"Murray!" I called. "Go see what's happening over there."

He returned quickly. "Things have gone badly for Capt. Creagh, Sir. He's sent for help and LT Godard's company is going. Moving out in 30 minutes."

"Well if it's to be a fight, they'll need us. Grab four of the doolies and two of our mules. See if the commissary officer has any pack saddles, we can't take the ambulance. I'll get the supplies."

Thirty minutes later, we were on the road. A second runner had come in from Creagh. Mohmands were crossing the river. Falling back to Dakka was not an option or it would require his little force to fight in a running battle they could not win. He was looking for a defensible position and going to hold on awaiting help.

Hopefully, our little force would be able to extricate Creagh. We were but one company of the "Fighting 5th", one company of Mhairwara infantry and a squadron of the 10th Bengal Cavalry. Capt. Strong of the 10th was in command and Capt. Trotter, the Political Officer, accompanied us. He would be trying to figure out why the Mohmands had crossed the river and then trying to explain it to Colonel Barnes.

The goat path through the Kam Dakka Pass was indeed difficult and treacherous. It took hours of climbing and the mules, sure footed as they are, were having great difficulty. The infantry was being held up by the need to keep the column together.

The order finally came back to the cavalry and packs that the infantry was pressing on and they were to come up as soon as they could. We were getting near Kam Dakka.

"Murray," I called. "Grab a medical bag. We're going with the 5th. Have the doolies bring the mules on."

Murray and I, each loaded with bags of medical supplies scrambled after the infantry, trying to close the gap from where we were in the rear of the column to the front. We passed through the Mhairwara and as we caught the coat tails of the 5th, I could hear firing to our front.

We stopped, looking down toward the river. To our left was the river and next to it what appeared to be a small graveyard and in it about one hundred and a half soldiers of the Mhairwara fighting for their lives. On the plain to the front and the hills surrounding were thousands of Mohmands. The firing from within the graveyard was intermittent. It was now three in the afternoon and surely their ammunition was running low.

73

The few soldiers in khaki in the graveyard, many with bandages visible, were in stark contrast to the turbaned natives in many colours with their red and white banners, pressing within a few yards of the miserable stone wall of protection.

Capt. Strong took all this in in a moment. "Godard, get your company ready to move. We're going in." Turning to the Mhairwara commander, he ordered them to cover the 5th from the hillside and protect their flanks as they advanced. Sending a runner back to LT. Pollack with the cavalry squadron, he ordered them up as quickly as possible. "Tell them to pitch in for the graveyard when he gets here," he told the runner.

Seeing me, Strong came over. "Doctor, best if you stay here with the Mhairwara Company."

"No, Sir, I'm with the 5th."

"Good for you, Doctor. Godard, you ready?"

"Yes, Sir. On your order."

"Right then, all those turbaned bastards are looking at the graveyard. We're going right down the trail. It's sunken and will keep us partially hidden. When we hit the plain, I want to break straight through. No stopping. Understand?"

"Yes, Sir," replied Godard.

I could see Godard was in his element.

"Doctor, I want you in the middle of the company. Stay with the pack, no matter what happens."

In a moment we were off. Moving as quickly as we could down through the rocky trail. I realized that even with all the noise of battle below that the noise of a company on the move was suddenly deafening. Even the click of rifle slings sounded like gunshots. Would the noise give us away before we reached our goal?

When we reached the bottom, the company reformed to change. Murray and I stood to the rear. The word came and we were off. Bayonets fixed and a wild, unexplained yell and we started to cut through the band of Mohmands. The unexpected charge from the rear instantly threw them into confusion. The Mohmands suddenly found themselves moving to the right, away from an unexpected enemy. A moment's hesitation on their part gave our little company its chance to run for the rock wall of the graveyard. But it was only a few seconds delay. We were but halfway and the bullets started coming our way. The Mohmands were not going to let us to our goal if they could.

As we closed to the graveyard we could hear a cheer from the defenders. That's when the terror struck. Murray was ahead of me when he went down in a heap. I nearly stumbled over him, reaching down, I grabbed him by his braces with my left hand, trying to pull him up. In my right hand was my Webley.

Murray scrambled to his feet, we were already yards behind the company. I have an impression even today of a face, a turban and a sabre. I fired over Murray's left shoulder as I pulled him along. The face was now red. To our front, between us and the wall were two more warriors. I fired at the one on the right but both figures fell. Behind the one on my left stood Godard with pistol in hand. Murray and I scrambled over the wall.

"Thought we'd lost you, old boy" smiled Godard. "Do try to keep up next time, eh?"

"I'll leave no man behind, Godard."

"Hmm, as you like. Wounded are over there by the riverbank."

As Murray and I went to the riverbank, Murray walked in front. He turned to face me. "Thank you, Sir. Sorry I stumbled."

"Not a problem. You'd do the same."

We started tending to the wounded. A few minutes later, we heard another cheer from the defenders. The charge of the 5th had disorganized the attackers, now Lieutenant Pollack and his squadron of the 10th had arrived. Capt. Strong ran out from the defences and regaining the horse he'd left with them, led the 10th Bengal Cavalry in a charge that cleared the plain and drove the Mohmands into the hills.

The Mhairwara Company in the pass entrance continued to hold on. Both the old and new defenders of the graveyard gathered dead and wounded and headed to join them. Murray and I could do little until we could stop at the pass. Captain Strong's charge had given us the chance to evacuate the graveyard but his orders had been to hold the pass.

As we gathered at the entrance to the pass, Strong started to deploy his force to hold it. What ammunition that was available was shared but Murray had been right. The only unit with a full load of ammunition was now the 5th who Strong placed in the forward position. While I attended to the most severe cases, Murray helped the walking wounded.

We had hardly ensconced ourselves in the entrance to the pass than the Mohmands returned from the far hills. They swarmed into the graveyard and started climbing the hills to our right and left where they would be able to fire down into our position. Captain Strong was about to deploy his Mhairwara company as skirmishers on the hillsides when the "Thunder of the Gods" erupted below us. It was artillery shells falling on the Mohmands in the graveyard! What a wonderful sight! A spontaneous cheer rose from the soldiers around me. Mohmands scattered in all directions. Anywhere they grouped, the shells sought them out. Once again, the Mohmands fled to the hills. Those in the graveyard tried to swim the river and I saw a dozen banners along with many turbans floating. Some drowned. Some made the crossing.

The two mountain guns we saw in the distance were supported by a company of infantry and advanced a few hundred yards at a time. It was soon clear that the Mohmand attackers were broken, at least for the moment.

Major Dyce of the Royal Artillery had arrived with two cannon and a company of the 12th Foot. As he joined us, he took quick evaluation of our circumstances. We were still receiving sporadic fire from the hillsides, we were low on ammunition, had no forage for the animals, no water for man or horse and Creagh's men had been fighting for 12 hours.

Taking command, as the senior officer present, Major Dyce ordered a withdrawal to Dakka. A most prudent decision.

The column, of necessity, moved slowly. The doolies could not move quickly with their human cargo and the mules and horses had a tough go of it. We were constantly under fire. We arrived back at the safety of Dakka with the setting sun. One of the mountain guns leading the way, the other to our rear. The gunners, with their cannon packed on mules, had saved us, surely.

But best of all, there sitting at a table in my office, smoking a pipe and drinking a whiskey with the Surgeon Major sat Sutter.

Chapter 9

"Sutter" I cried! "I was worried about you! Glad you are alright!"

"Worried about me?" exclaimed Sutter. "Look at yourself. You're a mess. Tough go? Here, sit down, let me get you one of your Surgeon Major's whiskeys."

"Can't, we've wounded to look after. Just walked in to inform the Doctor here."

"Nonsense," said the Surgeon Major of the 10th, rising from his desk. "I'm on my way to the ward right now. Take a moment. You do look like hell, you know. Sit for 10 minutes, then, come over. One tends to make mistakes when overtired. Don't want any of that." And with that, he left the office.

"Now sit and have a drink, John. Been up at Kam Dakka?"

Taking the whiskey, I sat in a chair and looked at Sutter. Now that I took the time, he looked quite worn out also, even if the uniform had been cleaned up.

"Yes," I replied. "Bit of a go. We did alright though."

We sat for some minutes and I enjoyed the calm and the silence.

I finally broke the silence.

"Sutter, I killed a man today, maybe two. One I'm sure of, the other, well, he went down but I feel he's dead too. Had to be done, you see." I sighed and went on. "I mean, it was them or me as they say in those penny dreadfuls. But what I don't understand is I don't really feel bad about it. I think I should, but I don't."

"John, it's not like they were good people or your friends. They were trying to kill you for heaven's sake."

"But they may have been good people, really, in their own way. I guess I'm a bit confused right now."

"All I can tell you, John, is you did the right thing. You survived and you took care of the other survivors."

"But I haven't asked where you've been. You're days overdue and should be at Jamrud, not here. What happened?"

"Not much," he replied. There was another moment's silence while he leaned back and put his boots on the table. "We left Jamrud and headed north, crossed the river and then west, making what we thought was a large loop. What happened was that the Mohmands started spilling out of the hills behind us. We couldn't get back the way we'd come. It was obvious that they had to be gathering for a reason. I had to keep moving northwest to try and stay unseen and got around them. By the time we found an opening, we were well west of Kam Dakka. I was able to ford the river about six miles west of here and made straight for Dakka. We arrived about two hours after your relief column left. Wired my report to Jamrud, borrowed a fresh horse and went back out on a little scout of my own."

"Scout of your own? What for? You couldn't have been any help to us."

"No, but I could be of help to us!" he declared, pointing his finger to me and then himself.

"Ah! The treasure! I should have known," I smiled and shook my head.

Sutter took his boots down and leaned across the table. "I've found a second Roman cross further up the same trail! Now will you believe me?"

I pondered this new information for a few moments. "Well, it certainly is now possible. Surely worth a look. When do we go?"

"Don't you have wounded to look after?" he smirked.

"Yes," I said, suddenly coming back to the moment. I took my last swallow and stood to go.

"See you tomorrow, John. I'm to bed. We can lay our plans then."

Unfortunately, the following morning we were occupied in loading to deport with the convoy at 7. As we left the gates of Dakka on route back to Jamrud, Sturt rode up to me. The two of us spent time trying to plan a campaign of discovery, but once we arrived at Jamrud, the business of the army, and for me, the business of opening the clinic absorbed all of our time.

Within a week or two of our return to Jamrud, my little clinic was open. At first there were few takers among the local populace. That, I was sure would come in time as we built the trust of the locals.

Murray and Malalai were constant companions. Each day I would receive two or three hospital assistants and a writer from the infirmary to help at the clinic. They arrived after morning sick call and we would journey to our little clinic tucked under the walls of the fort. For six hours each day, we would treat all who came, few as they were. In the second week of our operation, the flood tide came. Word had spread that treatment could be had at the clinic by the English Doctor and for no cost. I finally had to close each night at sundown and still there would be a line. The next morning those same people would be in the same line, waiting our arrival.

Malalai was a God-send. Her English improved with each day and she appeared at my elbow whenever I needed her help, as if, by magic. I found myself relying on her more and more.

It was mid-May before we knew it and Sutter and I had not been able to plan a way to get to Dakka again when the news arrived. There might be a chance of peace.

Yakub Khan wanted to negotiate peace because the Russians had let him down. The Tsar had decided that relations with England were more important that supporting a petty despot. By the end of May, the "Treaty of Gandamak" was signed. The treaty gave us control of the Khyber Pass and Kurram Valley, allowed a telegraph line to Kabul and put a British resident there to operate Afghanistan's foreign affairs. It also set a payment system to Yakub Khan by the Indian government.

On the first of June, Arty arrived in Jamrud, having taken a short furlough. Everyone was excited about peace. But what would happen to me and the treasure? Would we have time to find it before moving back to India? Sutter, Arty and I decided we must act now, and so, with a week's leave in our pockets, we mounted and well armed, we headed to

Dakka. The Regimental Surgeon, Armistead, agreed to run the clinic in my absence and Commissary O'Rourke, as always, saw to it that the three of us were well supplied.

Much against the advice of Murray and Malalai, we left, without escort, for Dakka. Our journey to Dakka was amazingly uneventful. The road was well travelled by columns of soldiers in good humour, looking forward to a return to India and relief from the heat of the Afghan summer. Still, there was the occasional shot from the hillsides, from those who either didn't know or didn't care that the two enemies were at peace.

At Dakka, we spent the night and the next day made off for the trail where Sutter had found the crosses.

"It's a theory," said Sutter. "I think that because the crosses were in each corner of the map that it stands for an even distance between the crosses. The second cross was about 3 miles from the first, so perhaps the 3rd is 3 miles from the second."

"Or perhaps it's double the miles from the first," said Arty.

"Or maybe you missed the second and actually found the third," I chimed in.

"You bastards just won't let a man dream, will you?" Sutter replied.

It was a good six miles from the main Dakka-Jalalabad road that we turned off to the north; another 3 miles brought us to the first cross. We dismounted to inspect it.

"It's definitely a Roman cross and quite old. Look at how the weather has worn the edges smooth. If we only knew it was the right one," mused Arty.

"Oh, it's the right one. I know it!" said Sutter. "It has to be."

I could feel the adrenaline surge as I slapped Sutter on the back. "You're right. I'm convinced. Which way to the next one?"

"Now look. Gents. I've been up here before. We're in bad country and we're alone. No column to save us if we should get into a tight spot. Watch your surroundings all the time and don't get fixated on the trail. Watch the hillsides."

Sutter's warning brought me back to reality with a sudden thud. He was right. This was not just a ride in the park.

We continued our journey up the trail, and as promised, about 3 miles ahead, was another cross chiselled in the stone along the side of the road. We inspected it briefly and went on. About a mile further and we came to a fork in the trail.

"Now what?" said Arty.

"Hold on," whispered Sutter. "Listen, rider coming from behind us. Quick! Around behind those rocks. Watson, you're horse holder. Arty, with me."

As Arty and Sutter dismounted, I led their horses further back and they moved to where they could see the trail while laying on their stomachs. I cursed my luck for being horse holder and not where I could see.

I could now clearly hear horses from the trail. I saw Sutter and Arty whisper to each other and raise their carbines. Both carbines barked at once, and then both men slid down toward me. Arty ran left and Sutter right. Sutter held a hand up telling me to stay where I was, as the two both ran up to higher ground. No sooner did they reach it, they fired again. Once more they descended and running back to their original spot, fired a third time. Now they screamed some gibberish I couldn't understand and fired a fourth round, but this time in the air. They yelled again and stood up looking back down the trail. Laughing jovially they started back down to where I held their mounts.

"What the devil is the matter with you two and who were you shooting at?"

"Nothing the matter with us, old boy. But Godard is having a bad day," said Arty, laughing again.

"Godard? You didn't shoot him?"

"No," said Sutter. "But I don't think he'll be following us anymore today. We just shot over him and yelled so he'd think it was tribesman. He and his pack mule took off back down the trail as fast as they could go"

Sutter took a breath and thought a moment. "That damned Enderby sent him out here alone to follow us. Godard should know better. We probably did him a favour by sending him back to Dakka."

"What do we do now?" I asked. "We've a fork in the trail and we don't want to split up."

"I vote we go right," said Arty. "Sutter, what about you?"

"Right works for me. If we don't find anything in 3 miles, we'll come back."

And so we were off on the wrong trail. Three hours later, we were back at the spot where we had turned right and by now night was falling. Finding a spot off the trail we camped for the night. We did not allow ourselves a fire, afraid we would draw attention. We grained and watered our horses and spent a most uncomfortable night either trying to sleep on the rocks or standing watch in 3 hour shifts.

Next morning we continued up the left fork.

"I wonder if Godard will be back?" I asked Arty.

"Doubt it. He doesn't know exactly where we're going and for all he knows, those 'tribesmen' he ran into may have done us in."

"You can bet he's waiting at Dakka," chimed in Sutter.

Three miles further along we came to the third Roman cross. There was now no doubt. This was the trail taken by Demetrios over two hundred years ago.

We sat for a pipe and each tried to make believe he was not excited. We were close now. Would the treasure be there and would we find it?"

We re-mounted and started forward on the trail again. We had gone but half the expected distance when Arty reigned up and stopped.

"Smell it?" he queried.

"What?"

"Wood fire. Someone's nearby," he warned. "Stay here, I'm going up on that hill." With that he handed me his reigns and started scrambling up the hillside. I could see him pull out his binoculars and scan the distance for a moment. Then, keeping low, he hurried down and re-joined us.

"We're done for now, fellows," he panted. "Over this little rise in the trail, the ground falls off to a little valley, and in it must be a thousand Mohmands. Gathering of some sort. Must be 50 banners. All gathered around a single tent."

"We can't go back now," cried Sutter. "We're too close."

"And I say dying finding a treasure is not worth it," spat Arty. "That treasure has been there over 200 years, another few days or months, won't matter. You know the Mohmands won't care about Yakub Khan's peace treaty if they see us here. John, what do you say?"

"I say we come back again. Better alive and poor than dead and rich."

And so we started our journey back. Sutter was morose and would not say a word until late that night as we entered Dakka Fort.

"You Gentleman were right," he said as we left the horses to be stabled. "Let's get a drink and plan what to do next."

As we entered the officers' mess, who should we see but Godard, sitting alone in a corner, brooding over a glass.

"Godard, old man," bellowed Sutter. "How wonderful to see you. What brings you this way?"

Godard nearly knocked the table over, spilling his glass as he jumped to his feet.

"Sturt, I thought you were, uh, I thought you had gone to Peshawar or somewhere. What ever are you doing here?"

"That was quick," whispered Arty in my ear.

"Just doing the rounds, needed some time to ourselves, you know. Well let me replace that drink. Seen any excitement lately? No? Well, probably nothing going on right now. Have a seat, man."

Pulling chairs up to the table we sat down and ordered drinks. His face was starting to flush as the realization of what had happened set in. Initially he had thought we'd been overpowered by the force he had escaped. Now he realized his mistake. We were the force he'd escaped.

Sutter made light chatter while we drank. Arty and I said nothing. Finally, Godard got up to leave.

"Going already? Well good night then," said Sutter. Then, as Godard reached the door, Sutter called out. "Oh, and Godard, do tell Colonel Enderby we send our best, good lad."

Godard merely turned and left the room.

"You know Sutter; you don't poke a lion cub with a stick. He just might turn on you," I said.

"John. John. You worry too much. He now knows we're watching him. He even believes we tried to kill him. He can't be sure we missed on purpose. He's going to be very careful from now on."

"We'd best be the careful ones," said Arty. "I'm all in. See you in the morning."

Next morning we returned to Jamrud.

The moment I returned, I was overwhelmed by work. The heat of the summer was upon us and the sick list increased with the heat. I was forced to reduce the clinic hours to six a day or I and my assistants should have no rest whatsoever. Malalai had greeted me warmly on my return and without my seeming to even notice it was she with me all the time. She was running errands, cleaning, cooking, and helping at the clinic. I started to rely on her more and more.

Word came down on the 21st that the 5th Fusiliers were to march on the 23rd for India, back to Chuagi, but Sturt and I were not to go with the regiment. I was detailed to the hospital at Peshawar and Sturt to the General Staff. It was a mixed blessing. It kept us within range of the treasure but Enderby was at Peshawar as was Godard, who had been made an aide-de-camp. At least Arty would be there with is detachment of the 18th Bengal Cavalry. But what about the clinic? And Malalai?

I realized I didn't want to lose her. She was like my little sister, I thought, or was she more? I wasn't sure how I felt now that we would be separated. We never talked of anything more than work but somehow I knew there was more there. Was it love? I sat in my quarters that night and thought for a long time. By the time I'd finished my pipe, I knew what I had to do. It was indeed a kind of love, but not that special kind that makes you say, "This is love."

The best thing for all would be to leave her in Jamrud. She now had skills and could be retained by the Army to assist in the infirmary. So it was that the morning of the 23rd we left for Peshawar with the 5th. Sturt, Murray and I to stay there and the 5th to move back to its garrison.

Early that morning, I had gone to see Malalai. She would not look at me nor say a word. I tried desperately to tell her how much I appreciated her and all her help and explain how important she was to the infirmary and the clinic. All I got were silent tears in return. Assembly sounded and as I left her hut, a sinking feeling overwhelmed me. Drawing a deep breath, I marched for the formation.

It was a very short march to Peshawar and I was soon at the hospital. It held well over 100 beds and was quite modern by Army standards. I was assigned a rounds schedule and all the first day found myself looking for Malalai at my elbow. It was a sad day.

Chapter 10

The summer of 1879 was hot and long. Sickness among the troops kept the hospital near capacity but supplies reached us in good time and overall Peshawar was not a bad assignment.

Arty and Sutter and I met frequently. Arty seemed to have the most boring job. His assignment as escort detachment kept him busy but in an uninspiring way. Spit and Polish became his life.

Sutter was occupied with planning. "What if this happens? What if that happens? And what if nothing happens?" was what he called his job.

Enderby had stopped by the hospital several times over the course of the summer. He would always seek me out and make a little small talk. He did not have a winning personality and, of course, I didn't trust him at all.

Godard would never say a word to me. In fact, whenever he saw any of us, he would always turn and go another way. We three friends chaffed to find a way to get back to Dakka together.

Finally, in late August, we agreed that Sturt should go alone to Dakka. In his position as a planner, he had need of first hand information as to the status of all the tribes in the Khyber Pass area. Word had been reaching the headquarters of much discontent among the Afridis, Shinwaris and Mohmands. Evidently, Yakub Khan was receiving monies from the British government but not passing a fair share down to the tribes as agreed. Sturt would take a small detachment and test the water among the tribes. We agreed that if he had the opportunity to look for the fourth cross he should. So, the last week of August he started for Dakka.

Terrible news reached us on the 4th of September. Unpaid Afghan regiments had run amuck in Kabul the day before. They had murdered the British Consul, Major Cavagnari and all his party and were threatening Yakub Khan. The war had been reignited.

That afternoon, Sutter appeared at the hospital. He had just returned from his intelligence gathering mission.

"I can only stay a moment, John. I've got to get back to headquarters. Hopefully we'll be bringing a sizeable force from India. Including the 5th, I hope."

"I can be ready in an instant," I said.

Calm down, John. The Army never moves that quickly," laughed Sutter.

"Are we going straight to Kabul?"

"Doubt it. We're strongest in the Kurram Valley where your cousin is. They'll probably be the ones to take Kabul. Ours will be a supporting attack. I'll let you know more on that as I can." With that he was gone to report in to headquarters.

Late that evening as I was about to turn in, a knock came on my door. It was Sutter and Arty.

"We came to drink your whiskey, John."

"On the table, Arty. What's going on that I'm honoured by such a nocturnal visit?"

"Treasure," sighed Arty, sitting on my bunk, glass in hand.

"Needed to fill you two in on what I found on my ride. Or more importantly, what I didn't find," said Sutter, sitting on the table. "I was able to get past the third cross and on down into the valley, I'm sure my detachment thought I was crazy. I took them up the trail allegedly looking for Mohmands to talk to. We found plenty, sitting on the rocks above us. But since we were nominally at peace, they watched but held their fire. We got down in the valley without incident but at around three miles, I could not find the marker." Sutter became frenzied. Standing up, he started pacing up and down the tiny room, clasping and unclasping his hands.

"I trooped that detachment up and down the road a dozen times. They thought I'd lost my mind. The Mohmands gathered in small groups and watched. I'm sure they were convinced we were plotting something. Finally I could do nothing but move on back toward the main road, the Mohmands starting moving along with us. They started taking pot shots from the hillsides. Fortunately, we made it back without any casualties."

"We need to all go back and try to find it. It's got to be there, my friend," said Arty.

"Not much chance of that now, I'm afraid, the whole frontier is on fire. We've got to wait for things to calm down again."

All we can do now is our jobs and wait," I added. "But we don't do any lone reconnaissance like our friend Godard. Anyone shoots at us, it will be for real."

So each of retuned to our respective jobs, setting aside the treasure and hoping our efforts would help bring a peace to the area.

For me, the months of September, October and November dragged. The wounded, flowing back to Peshawar, were a constant reminder that the war was active and Lord Roberts was moving toward Kabul. Yakub Khan, as it turned out, was not involved in the murder of Major Cavagnari, but he was a weak ruler as well as corrupt. Yakub Khan had not realized that he had neither the leadership nor the charisma to hold his tribes together. Add to that his failure to pay his soldiers and giving Afghan territory to the British, which inflamed the tribes, and he was done. By the end of October, Roberts had taken Kabul and on the 28th day of October, Yakub Khan abdicated but that didn't stop the fighting. The lack of a strong Afghan leader left dozens of tribes each going their own way. Roberts executed 47 men accused of participating in the death of the British Consul and his men, while just, this action further inflamed the situation.

By December, confusion still was the order of the day in Afghanistan and the Indian government finally agreed to send a reserve division in to the fight. The second division being needed in Afghanistan and off the supply line, the Reserve Division would take up the duty of securing the lines of communication.

Just before Christmas, Sutter and Arty came to see me in my quarters.

"The 5th has been ordered to Peshawar, John. Odds are it will move on from there."

"If the 5th is to see action, you and I need to be there, Sutter!"

"You're right there. Well, John, you're re-assigned to the 5th. They'll be passing through day after tomorrow so have your kit ready. We're headed

94

to Jamrud first, then on to Jalalabad, is what I think. More convoy duty looks like. Good Night, John. Come along, Arty, your horses will be missing you."

As promised, the next morning I had my orders to re-join the 5th. It seems that in all the confusion associated with re-mobilizing the Army, Colonel Enderby had not paid attention to either me or Sturt and so lost us, at least for the moment.

Sturt and I re-joined the 5th as the convoy stopped at Peshawar overnight. It was good indeed to be back with the men I respected and trusted. I had learned so much so far. Even not to doubt Surgeon Major Bennett. He was truly a caring and gifted doctor, even if a little tipsy at times.

The march as far as Jamrud was uneventful. Once again, Murray and I were eating the trail dust and wondering if we would ever again be clean.

As we entered Jamrud, the regiment was tolled off to camp below the north wall of the fort. As soon as I was able, I found myself going in search of Malalai. Why I did so was plain to me. I cared for her very much and wanted to know that she was all right, that she had been treated well since I left. I found her in the native clinic. She looked wonderful and on seeing her, I felt wonderful.

She was talking to a local at the front desk as I entered. At first, she didn't notice me, so intent was she in the discussion.

"Miss Malalai, come here, I need you," I said in my sternest voice.

"Yes, Doctor," she responded and looking up, saw me. Her grin was a delight and she ran over to me. Suddenly catching herself, she stopped just as she reached me and looked at the ground.

"You wanted me, Doctor?"

"I've come to see my favourite assistant, Malalai. How are you?" I smiled and reached down to lift her chin so she would look at me. Her eyes were watery. She grinned and wiped them with a towel. "It is good to see you, doctor. You have come back to us?"

"No, just going onto Jalalabad. But I could not go past here and not stop to see how you were. You're doing well I see."

"Yes. The doctors are all good to me and Mr Moyer give me English teaching ever day, He is kind."

"Excellent. I'm glad you're doing so well. I must go now but when I come back through, I'd like to check on you again, if you would permit me?"

"Of course, Doctor. I would be very happy."

With that I left, pleased that Malalai was going so well. The next day we left again for Jalalabad, where we were to spend a long, cold winter.

Chapter 11

Jalalabad was a large fort by our standards, a major re-supply point. It was early January when I, Murray and Sturt and a quartering party arrived. For the first week we were occupied arranging for the arrival of the rest of the 5th. They had been delayed at Jamrud and there was talk of the headquartering there instead. As it finally ended up, we had two companies at Jalalabad and the preponderance of the 5th at Jamrud, though on many occasions in the next few months, most of the 5th would be at Jalalabad due to escorting convoys.

The convoys were constantly under attack. Through the months of February, March and April, Lord Roberts was trying to settle the Afghan tribes, but without an Afghan leader who was both strong and friendly to us, his task was nigh impossible. The constant work kept me from any thought of the treasure, but I could tell that Sutter was constantly trying to devise a plan to once again search for it. Godard too, was ever present company. He had been reassigned to the regiment with duty at Jalalabad. This, I'm sure, was arranged by Colonel Enderby. Where I or Sutter went, there would appear our silent friend, watching.

In late April, things were still in quite an uproar everywhere. It seems that a Mulla Khalil was calling for a "holy war" and was assembling all the riff-raff of the frontier to his standard. Khalil had a large number of Safis, and with them he occupied Besud and Goshta. It was Sutter who let me know things were about to get worse.

"Colonel Rowland will be here tomorrow," he said, as we walked the parade ground. "He's on his way to Safed Sang, with the Mulla making trouble we can expect some attacks on our communications lines. They say General Doran may move his headquarters here. We may be in for a small campaign to clean out this fellow. Better than just going back and forth up the road."

"How have your recommendations to protect the commissariat stores faired?" I asked.

"Fools won't bring up a proper security force for it or move it closer to the fort. They don't want to "smell the cattle". Tell me, Watson, what do you do with people like that?" Sutter's words were to prove prophetic.

On the following day, Colonel Rowland arrived with an additional 300 bayonets of the 5th. It was decided that they would rest here at Jalalabad before going on.

We had a jovial time that first night. Early May was a genial month. Warmer weather, snows melting, and what green the country had starting to show. Local villagers were starting to prepare the rice paddies for the planting season. But with the improved weather had come more raids on the lines of communication. It would soon be campaign time.

The next day was a busy one. I spent the morning attending to the usual complaints of soldiers on the march, blisters, corns and boils. I gave Murray some time off to visit with friends he hadn't seen in months and instead he spent his afternoon operating a cleaning station for the men of the 5th where they could have their leather braces and uniforms cleaned by the natives while they had hot water to bathe and shave.

It was late that evening, nigh onto three in the morning and most officers had long left the mess. Colonel Rowland, Sturt, I and two or three others remained at a table playing cards. We were discussing the coming campaign season and wondering if Ayub Khan could be brought under control quickly when the officer of the day rushed in.

"Is Colonel Rowland here?" he called from the doorway.

"Here, Lieutenant. What can I do for you?"

"Sir, the General's compliments and he wished you to fall out the battalion. The commissary stores and cattle yard are being attacked and need immediate assistance."

"Right. Go find Major Tucker, lieutenant, should be in quarters. Sturt, your men too." Turning to the table, he called to a young lieutenant, "Withers have the bugler sound assembly. Off now, quick!"

"Doctor," he said. "Gather your men and follow as quickly as you can. Hustle now. Can't let these locals have the cattle."

I ran from the mess and to the hospital calling for Murray, an ambulance and doolie-bearers. It took not more than twenty minutes for the mules to be harnessed, my horse saddled and supplies loaded. Yet we were still ten minutes behind the battalion.

I headed west on the road toward the cattle yard, it was just after four in the morning.

We caught up to the battalion at the cattle yard and fell in at the tail end of the column. As we did, a detachment of cavalry, maybe 20 sabres, passed us headed for the front of the column. I spurred forward with them and was soon up with Sturt's company. I reigned up here.

"Do we know what's happened? That cattle yard is awfully empty!"

"Looks like they've taken a thousand head, overwhelmed the guard detachment just like I feared. About 180 sheep taken as well. They can't move too fast, we'll catch them. Looks like they've headed toward Laghman. We can't be more than 30 minutes behind them."

I stayed with Sturt for the better part of the morning. About 8 we could hear firing to our front.

"Best get back to the ambulance, Doctor. Looks like the beggars are going to fight a holding action at Darunta gorge. They're liable to hold us up a bit."

From where we were in the rear, we watched the battalion form in line with a company in reserve along with the cavalry. (Cavalry being of no use in the gorge.) Even from where I was, the positions of the Ghilzais were easy to pick out. The black powder muskets sent large clouds of white smoke in the sky, revealing their positions in the rocks. I counted about 60. It would be hard work for the skirmisher to root them out. If we'd had mountain guns, we'd have made short work of it for the Ghilzais would not stand to artillery. As it was, each rock on the hillsides over the gorge would have to be fought for.

I determined to move forward with the ambulance. We had a 35 gallon water keg and there was a stream to our right rear. As the skirmishes inched forwards, I had the doolie-bearers supplement the bhisti's filling water bottles among the soldiers.

Finally, after almost 2 hours of fighting, the path through the gorge was taken and we moved through. By now, however, we were far behind the cattle and moving further from any support. The soldiers were in light marching order; braces, haversacks, ammunition bag, water bottle, mess tin, blanket and glengarry, bayonet and rifle. We had not wagons save the ambulance, no food nor extra water. To continue after the Ghilzais would have been folly with so small and ill supported a force. We returned to Jalalabad.

The Ghilzais had made off with 800 cattle. We were able to collect 200 on the return and about 60 of the sheep. And the self-satisfied smirk on Sturt's face lasted a week.

I felt somewhat sorry for the villagers between Jalalabad and Daruta. Over the next few days, patrols exacted a fine of 4000 rupees from the villagers, for neither reporting Ghilzais in the area or trying to delay their escape. Had they made the report they would have their villages threatened with destruction by the Ghilzais, but because they had not reported, we took their money. A sad predicament.

On the 9th, when Colonel Rowland thought he would continue to Safed Sang, he was ordered to remain at Jalalabad and await General Doran. There was to be a move to put down Mulla Khalil in Besud.

Chapter 12

With the arrival of General Doran was the pleasant surprise of Arty and his detachment of the 18th Bengal Cavalry.

He caught up with me down by the stables, for while I had a native to take care of my horse, I had always enjoyed grooming and caring for Emmett myself, whenever time permitted. I've always believed in the bond between horse and rider. It's something special, more than once I've seen a fine mount stand guard over his fallen master or the tearful goodbye of horseman for his lost companion.

At any rate, that's where Arty found me, brushing Emmett and talking to him like he could understand.

"He has no idea what you're saying, old man. He's just waiting for a treat. Sorry job of grooming, afraid you'd never make it in the cavalry."

"Arty!" I exclaimed, shaking his hand. "Just popping in for a visit?"

"Escort again. The brass always likes the native horse along. Makes them feel more secure. Been on a ride?"

"Chasing some cattle thieves like this is the wild west of America or something. But come on, let's go find Sutter. He'll be delighted to see you."

"Want to talk to you about this bloody treasure no doubt. You know, John, if there is a treasure, it's probably been found a couple of centuries ago, and if it hasn't, it belongs to the church by rights. I've thought about that lately."

We left the stable and Arty insisted on checking on his picket line to see that his horses were being taken care of. I noticed he did not intrude on his sergeant's business but merely walked the line and kept going. "Good to let them know you trust them but you care enough to check," he said half nodding to himself. "Now where is Sutter's orderly room? Or perhaps he's already retired to the mess?"

"This time of day I'd say orderly room." And indeed, that is where we found him.

"Come in Arty, John, have a seat," grinned Sutter as we entered. "How good of you to stop by for out little foray. Cigars are in the box on the table, help yourself."

"With pleasure, old man," said Arty, opening the box and taking out two cigars. Handing one to me, he dropped into a chair by the table that served as Sturt's desk.

"What little foray are you talking about?" I asked.

"Seems the good General has decided to quash a Mulla named Khalil. This fellow has been gathering followers right across the river from here and causing problems, so we're going to stop him before he gets further along."

"Is it far?" asked Arty.

"No, look at this map."

The three of us stood to look at the map Sutter had on the wall.

"Here we are in Jalalabad," he tutored. "Just across the river is a triangle known as Basud. It sits between the Kabul and Kunar rivers. There are two paths that run north. One is along the Kunar River and goes past a place called Tokchi. The other goes over the Paikob Pass abut two miles to the west, and there is this long hill line that runs about 4 miles that separates them."

"The Tokchi Pass," he continued, sitting back down, "is pretty bad overall. Even infantry can only get through in single file, horses the same. Now Paikob is no problem."

"Well, this country out here," said Arty, pointing up at the flat area of Basud, "looks ideal for cavalry."

"Try it, my friend," laughed Sutter. "It's nothing but rice fields and this time of year they're flooded. Neither infantry nor cavalry cross them without getting shot to pieces. I surely don't want to try it."

"What kind of force are we facing?"

"Apparently, a sizable group of Safis. The General is holding onto the 5th and ordered the 4th Madras Infantry up. He's also ordered the locals to start building rafts for a crossing. The bridge has to be taken down before the spring flood waters arrive or they'll lose it. They'll put it back up when the waters go down."

Within a few days of our conversation, the 4th Madras arrived and on the 14th day of May, 200 of them were sent to the far side of the river to the fort of Pir Muhammad Khan, about ½ mile up from the bridgehead. This was done to assure the locals that we would protect them and to defend the north side for our crossing later.

The next few days were extremely busy. Fifty sabres of the Central India Horse, a unit my cousin had commanded in 1871, arrived and were sent to join Major Tyndall's force at Fort Pir Muhammad Khan. Then came the 9th Bengal Infantry to Jalalabad, along with the 12th Foot and four guns of I-A Royal Horse Artillery. We were becoming a sizable force.

On the 18th, Murray, I, three hospital assistants, a half dozen doolie-bearers and our little ambulance were ferried across the river with 200 rifles of the 5th, led by Colonel Rowland. The ambulance we would leave in Dabela by the bridgehead and use our four mules to pack in medical supplies.

The next morning at half four, we departed Dabela, leaving a small force to watch the stores. We were a force of over 500 bayonets, 80 sabres and two mountain guns. It always seemed to me odd and somewhat disconcerting, that mention was rarely made or record kept of the numerous commissary and medical department personnel that accompanied all the various expeditions during the war. And if little mention was made of these necessary auxiliaries to the force, none whatsoever was made of the bhistis or doolie-bearers and the like, although they all shared the hardships and the hazards. Perhaps someday the bhistis will get their due.

We were not long on the march, about an hour and a half, when a halt was called. We had travelled west up the right of the river and then turned north across the rice swamp.

I trotted Emmett up to the front of the column and on the hillside to our northeast I could make out General Doran and a small party. They appeared to be looking eastward. I sought out Sturt and asked if he knew what was happening.

"Seems there are about two thousand of those damned Safis to the east and they're headed to the south in small groups," he replied. "They're as close to Darunta and the bridgehead as we are! We've got to cut them off before they can get there. If they overrun the boys there, they can go on across the river all the way to Jalalabad and we'll be stuck over here."

"But aren't there sufficient men at Darunta?"

"Well. If they have improved their defences, they may be alright. Bradford said the Royal Artillery was putting two cannon at the bridgehead on our side of the river. Surely they can hold." But Sutter didn't sound convinced. Just then a rider could be seen racing down the hill. He rode straight to Colonel Dawson of the 1st Madras who was nearby in conference with Colonel Rowland.

The Lieutenant saluted as he reigned in his horse. "General's compliments, Colonel Dawson. The General says the Safis are headed straight towards us into the open ground. It doesn't appear they know we're here. He requests you form line of battle and prepare for an attack." With that, he was off again, riding for the hill to our front.

Dawson turned to the officers around him. "Rowland, take the left. Form three companies and refuse one to the left. The 12th will do the same on the right. I'll take the 1st and the 4th Madras in the centre. Lieutenant Bradford, I want your two cannon centred to the rear of the Madras. Colonel Martin, if you'll take the Central Horse to the left, that flank is very open, keep a lookout if the beggars try to come in that way. Use your own discretion if they fall back, you may be able to cut them off. Gentlemen, to your units please."

All saluted and rode post haste for their columns. I rode back to our little medical detachment as fast as I could go. I quickly told my men what was going on and we moved forward behind the second company of the 5th. It is astonishing how quickly a well trained force of soldiers can form to line of battle. Ahead of us, 120 men, bayonets fixed; to our left, another 60 ready to reinforce the line or defend against attack from the left. To our right, mules and cannon unlimbering in an instant and ready to fire. And so we waited, but not for long, for no sooner had we deployed than the first dark figures came over the hillside. A few at first, then hundreds. But they seemed to be confused by the sight of our little Army and were gathering up. They stood a good 1200 yards away and static, neither wanting to advance or retreat. We made the decision for them. The order was made to move forward. The entire formation advanced in unison; Infantry, Artillery, Cavalry. A wondrous sight to behold. We had closed about half the distance when the order to fire was given. Artillery and Infantry fire rained down on our enemy.

For a short while, the masses of turbaned men held their ground as the shells played back and forth across the front, the two gun crews working feverishly to support our soldiers across the entire area. But now it was the infantry fire that broke the Safis line.

The rifle fire from the 5th proved to be more than the Safis could stand and the enemy right began to flee. Like a house of cards, Mulla's army crumbled once their right collapsed, for the rest were in fear. Dawson seeing his chance, ordered the Central India Horse to overtake the enemy as they fled to the hills or to a small fort to their rear. The Horse swept down upon the fleeing throng with sabre and carbine. From where I sat on Emmett, I could see the Horse cut down our fleeing foe, creating havoc among their ranks.

We advanced again, and the Horse drew back to our lines. Those Safis in the hills melted away. The rest sought safety in the small fort. We stopped a few hundred yards from the fort while the cannon ripped holes in the walls and the towers. So far, I had had no work to do as we'd had but one soldier only slightly wounded. As the firing from the fort started to die off, the 5th advanced to storm the quadrangle and the artillery ceased its pounding. Colonel Rowland and the 5th swept through the fort, firing kept coming from the southeast tower. The guns were called on again to open a way in the wall of the tower and once breached, Rowland, Captain Kilgour, Colour Sergeant Wood and a few of the men stormed the tower, fighting hand to hand with bayonet and sabre.

Once the fighting died, I was busy indeed. Fortunately, we had no one killed, but Colonel Rowland and six soldiers had been wounded in taking the tower. Fortunately, the wounds were slight, most were made by sabres, and I had the privilege of seeing to Colonel Rowland.

The entire battle had lasted by an hour. And now, after destroying the remainder of the fort, we marched back to Dabela. It was only ten in the morning. The early afternoon found us back at Dabela and I left Murray to check supplies and see to the care of the men and mules while I went off to find Sturt. I came across McMullen first. His detachment had been left at Dabela and had spent the day acting as scouts, watching for the possible approach of Safis.

"Quite an adventuresome day you had, John. I hear you weren't kept busy though, professionally, that is."

"No, fortunately our injuries were few and none severe. Colonel Rowland and the 5th made an outstanding show of it. Very impressive. Have you seen Sturt?"

"Haven't, but we'll find him at sundown, never fear. He knows where the whiskey is kept," laughed Arty.

True to Arty's prediction, Sturt appeared later in the evening as we smoked cigars beneath the wall of the fort.

"Tomorrow is a day of rest evidently," said Sturt, walking up.

"Cigar?" I offered.

"Don't mind if I do."

"Do I take it from your remark that we've more to do afterwards?" Arty inquired.

"Two more forts to destroy to make sure the beggars get the idea. One called Azamulla Khan Kala and another at Danaras Khan, have to level them before we go back across the river."

"I hope the bridge is still standing by the time we have to re-cross," I observed. "The river is rising quickly."

"Engineer officers are afraid of the same thing. Let's hope there are plenty of rafts. Oh, and by the way John, the Colonel wants to see you. He's terribly grateful for your patching him up. Don't know why. Just a scratch after all."

"Quite a delicate operation, in fact," I said, striking a pose with my cigar. "Not one in a hundred surgeons could do so well."

We all laughed and enjoyed the evening. The next day, Colonel Rowland thanked me for being "Johnny on the spot" with the regiment and hoped we'd have a long affiliation. He was to be disappointed.

Chapter 13

On the following two days, we made the two treks. One to Azimulla Khan Kala and the other to Danaras Khan. Both forts were destroyed with minimal interference from the locals.

It was now time to re-cross the river. In the time we had spent destroying the forts, the last bridge had been swept away. We would now have to cross the raging river on rafts or swim the horses and elephants. The effort to cross took two days and was not without loss.

A rope was tied down stream between the two shores which were about 400 yards apart. Those who could swim well were given unrolled turbans and posted along the rope to catch those who might be swept along. All day on the 23rd, troops and equipage crossed under the cover of the cannons on the right bank. The Central India Horse crossed both ways time and again to swim horses and mules packed with equipment across. The cannon from the mule mountain battery were packed on elephants to keep them above the six foot deep waters and their mules swam across. As things will, with all the success, still, one artillery driver and a sowars horse were lost, swept past the catch line.

Our little ambulance had been loaded with cavalry saddles and rafted across to be reunified on the far side with our mules that were swum across by the Horse. This task I left to Murray. The 5th had been given the task of defending the re-crossing of the river and I had stayed with Sturt as our defensive perimeter had collapsed on itself, getting smaller and smaller as there were fewer and fewer soldiers to defend against attack. As night fell and operations had to cease, we were now but a single company of 65 men on the wrong side of the river. Sturt had now crossed also. Lt. Godard was the sole remaining officer and as much as I was uncomfortable with the situation, I also stayed. If an attack came, our little band would be sorely pressed and they'd have need of me.

Godard decided to make a show of things by stealing a well known tactic from history. Instead of refusing the use of campfires, which would give away our location and small strength, he instructed his sergeant to build a campfire for every two men and keep the fires burning all night. From a distance, in the dark, it appeared we had still a sizeable force on the left back of the river. I suppose I shall never know if the ruse worked or was necessary but we weren't abused except for the occasional pot shot out of the darkness and our picquets were quiet.

"Doctor, you really didn't have to stay here, you know. Nothing will happen and we'll cross in the morning."

"Perhaps, Godard, but one never knows what eventuality may occur."

We stood near the crossing site out of the firelight. Taking a hip flask out his haversack Godard offered me a drink.

"You know, Doctor," he said as he took a pull from the flask. "You really would be better served by paying more attention to who your friends are and who you support. Colonel Enderby could be very useful to your career. He isn't such a bad fellow."

"Truly," was all I could say. I stood for a moment, puffing on my cigar while I thought. Finally, I came to a decision.

"Godard, why are you supporting Enderby in his attempt to steal Sturt's map?"

Godard laughed for a moment and walked over to sit on a nearby rock.

"Let me put it to you this way, Watson. Violet was my fiancé when McMullen and Sturt showed up. We were to be married in about 6 months time. It took only 3 months for them to interfere and destroy my life. I don't wish them dead, you understand. But I want something that means a great deal to them taken away. It's really quite that simple. Vengeance!" He spat the last word with a hatred I had seen in few men, as he rose from his seat.

"But, how did you know about the map?" I queried.

"Oh," he murmured, setting back down. "That rumour has been around forever. And when Sturt's had a few, he can't keep a secret."

With that, a bullet splashed in the water near us and I could hear the report to our left.

"Blighters are not going to let us rest tonight, are they?" remarked Godard. "I'd best assure myself that the good sergeant is making the rounds. Do try to get some sleep, Doctor." So saying, he rose from the rock and started for the campfires. A few paces out, he stopped and turned back toward me.

"Do remember my advice, Doctor. Choose your friends and your battles carefully. Your decisions can have rather far reaching effect." He turned again and I was left to my own thoughts once more. At least now I knew the origin of the enmity between the three men.

By first light, we saw the return of 20 elephants to our side of the river and we loaded on them to leave Besud.

On our return to Jalalabad, we rested a day or two and Colonel Rowland and most of the 5th headed once again toward Safed Sang. Jalalabad was now General Doran's headquarters.

On the second morning after our return, Sturt approached me out on the parade grounds.

"Watson, old man, our chance has come. Be ready to move tomorrow. We've got our chance to go after the treasure. "

"How can that be? We're stuck here at Jalalabad."

"There is a large convoy due to reach Dakkar on the 6th. It's going to need extra escort because of the large amount of ammunition and new screw guns coming up to support Kabul. My company is being sent down to bring them to Jalalabad. I've asked for you to go along as well as Arty's detachment."

"You Devil, they approved it? And we go a week early?"

"Old Doran doesn't much care. Doesn't pay much attention to the details you know. As long as he's plenty of soldiers here to play with, he's happy."

"I'll be ready to move in the morning." I grinned. Then I thought, "Tell me, what about Godard? Where will he be?"

"Oh, his company is staying here. Part of my overall suggestion to Doran's aide. Companionable fellow, Major Baskerville likes things presented in neat, little packages. Do that and he'll agree to almost anything."

"You Devil," I repeated. "I marvel at your sagacity. Always find a way, don't you?"

"Always, Doctor. We march at five. 'Til the morning, then." And with a wave of his hand, he was off across the parade.

Chapter 14

It was the 27th of May, 1880, and unbeknownst to me, the search for the treasure was about to take a marked turn. As planned, we departed Jalalabad before the sun had risen over the eastern hillside. Our caravan marched the well travelled military road with but a few incidents, the flankers provided by Arty's detachment doing good duty. We reached Dakka on the 29th. This play by Sturt would leave us nine days in which to search for the treasure, assuming of course, that the locals didn't make noise and cause us problems. That night, Arty, Sutter and I gathered at the mess to plan our strategy for the coming campaign.

"Just how do you intend to explain our absence from Dakka?" I asked Sutter.

He swirled his whiskey in his glass as he drew another puff on his cigar. "Splendid thing, reconnaissance," he finally said. "Any hint of a rumour about Mohmands re-organizing and people want to know more about it."

"Of course, having extra officers, with experience of course, laying about the fort, gives you someone to send on a mission." Smiling to himself, he leaned back and took another puff.

"What rumour?" I asked. "I haven't heard anything about it."

"Seems we picked up some information on the march down here. Don't you know, old man?"

"But Sutter, you never told me about it."

Sturt looked at me and shook his head. Turning to Arty, he said, "A true babe in the woods.

116

How shall we ever be able to release him in the wild?"

The two of them had a hearty laugh and raised a toast to each other.

"John, old boy, he made it up for the brass, of course," whispered Arty in my ear.

The plan was suddenly clear. What a dolt I'd been. Of course Sturt would have had a plan to get us out of Dakka and into Mohmand territory.

We then discussed the make up of our little party. It was agreed that since we didn't know the exact location, nor did we know whether or if we would need tools to dig, we would need supplies and a pack mule.

"Do you think Murray is to be trusted?" asked Sturt.

"I'd trust him with my life," I replied.

"Good! We'll take him to take care of the mules. Two ought to do. Arty, do you have four men you can trust?"

"As the Doctor said, with my life."

"Good. We really don't know what the situation is with the Mohmands, so we'll bring a few along. Leave them at the second cross in case they're needed and take Murray with us into the valley. Six days rations ought to do. Your men ought to be safe at the hiding spot John used below the cross."

"If I'm going to risk a man's life, Sutter, I'm going to tell him why. I've got to explain this to Murray," I insisted.

Sutter thought for a moment, "You're right, John. If we find, no, when we find the treasure, we'll give him a small share. Agreed?"

Arty and I nodded. It was only fair.

We broke up late that evening, having discussed in detail what we would do for the next six days; eight would be the most that we could stretch our search out to. As we left the mess, I went in search of Murray. I found him doing his nightly check on the mules.

"Private Murray, I have something I want to discuss with you."

"Yes, Sir."

"Come over to the ambulance and have a seat on the tail board. I have something to discuss with you at length."

"Right, Sir. But I'll just stand here if that's alright."

Taking a deep breath, I launched into an explanation of the situations. Murray was incredulous at first; I could see it in his face. But as I laid out our series of adventures, I could see he was finally beginning to believe me. I explained everything, from the treasure to Godard to Enderby, to our search for the fourth cross.

"Well, Sir," he finally said. "I'm your man. I trust you and the other gentleman to give a fair amount. When do we go?"

"Tomorrow, early. Can you be ready? No more than two of our mules. Lieutenant McMullen will bring you a mount."

"I'll be ready, Sir."

I held out my hand to Murray. "Take it, Murray. We've an agreement among gentlemen."

"Aye, Sir," he said, taking my hand. "We're agreed."

As the morning sun rose, the eight of us departed Dakka Fort, in search of treasure.

We moved swiftly, for we knew our way and it was but a half day's journey to the second cross.

Arty had explained to his men that we were on a mission of importance that they would find rewarding but had not explained further. As we made our noon stop at the foot of the second cross, he explained to them that they were to wait there for our return but should they be discovered and threatened by Mohmands in force, not to await us but immediately return to Dakka.

Here we left also one of the mules with supplies for the four sowars and pressed on. By mid afternoon, we were at the third cross and looking down into the valley. We could see a good seven miles as the trail wandered through the valley and disappeared into the distant hills. This time there was no conclave of Mohmands.

We decided we would start by traveling the trail from one side to the other, searching both sides just as Sturt had done earlier. Perhaps because of the pressure of being watched by hostile tribesmen he had merely missed it. So we started down. By the time we reached the valley floor, we moved slowly, watching for the cross. The sun was starting to set and we decided to camp for the night. Dividing the watch up among the four of us, the first night passed uneventfully. Having watered and grained the animals, they were hobbled and allowed to graze for a short time. Once morning came, we allowed ourselves a small fire to cook and make tea. Then, having saddled and packed, we started on through the valley, crossing its whole length and back again. We could find no sign of the fourth cross. On returning to our original starting point in the late afternoon, we conferred on our next move.

"Perhaps the cross has been destroyed," ventured Arty.

"Or the trail is not where it used to be," I put in. "Though it seems the logical path through the valley."

"It must be here," stormed Sutter. "It must!"

"Well, I'll be damned if I know where," I jibed, and sitting upon some rocks, took to my pipe to try and think.

"We have to expand the search area." Sutter insisted and so, in an hour we were back out upon the trail. This time, Murray and I travelled about 200 yards to the right and Arty and Sutter 200 yards to the left. It was very slow going and we were only about halfway down the valley when darkness forced us to stop for the night.

The next morning found us continuing on our search. We could find nothing and by early evening we were back where we had camped the first night, no better for two wasted days of searching.

I now suggested we go back to the third cross and see if there was a clue there which would present itself. It turned out to be a fortuitous suggestion. We had been sitting on the hillside for about a half hour, having found no clue when Murray approached me.

"Sir, I was sitting here looking at the valley and I have an idea."

"All ideas are welcome, Murray," I said, reaching in my haversack for another cigar.

"Well Sir, you said we're looking for one of them Russian kind of crosses with those three bars on it, right?"

"Yes," I laughed, "but without much success." Striking a lucifer, I lighted my cigar while Murray appeared to be lost in thought. Finally he turned and pointed toward the valley which was below us.

"Well, the whole valley is one of them crosses, Sir. Ain't it?"

I sat stunned for a moment. Rising, I looked at the valley in the setting sun. He was right! The whole bloody valley was the cross. The trail that led straight from one end to the other was the upright and crossing it in three places were fingers of hills which formed the three cross members. The far and centre hills were almost perpendicular and the near crossed at an angle from left to right. That must be the solution!

"Arty! Sutter! Quickly before the light fades! Come here! Murray has solved it!"

Pointing to the valley, I outlined the orthodox cross for them. For a moment, we were ecstatic with joy. But then reality set in. A whole valley to search? And for a single casket of jewels? Where were we to start? Our depression quickly returned.

We each spent time that night trying to arrange in our minds how we could possibly search an entire valley. Was there an orthodox cross that also marked the spot? If so, where? We lay awake all night trying to come up with a solution to our problem. I was sitting with Arty as the sun was coming up, no closer to a solution than when the sun had gone down.

"You'd think these blasted priests would have made things a little easier for us laymen," fumed Arty.

"Well things that were obvious to them we may not even think of anymore," I ventured.

"Well it's not obvious to me."

I leaned back on the rocks and was watching the sun come up. I was suddenly tired. Trying too hard, I thought sun rise, or maybe son rise? I chuckled to myself. What did I know about a cross? Not much, surely. I was used to crucifixes more than crosses. Why were they different? I Know Miss Eileen had explained it to me. Let's see, upright and cross bar where Christ was nailed, of course. Then there is a small top cross where they nailed the notice INRI, Jesus, King of the Jews. The bottom crossbar was where they tied a person's feet. Most criminals were tied to the cross. The nailing of Christ was unusual. Tying a man to the cross, he actually drowned as fluids filled his lungs over the course of a day or so. Had to do with the position. Well, nothing in all that. I rose and started to walk around, looking out at the valley. Then it came to me. In a moment, I knew what it all meant.

"Arty! Sutter! Murray!" I called, half frantic with excitement. "I've got it! I know where to look!"

"Well don't just stand there, where do we look?" shouted Sutter.

"No fun if I just tell," I said strutting up and down, very proud of myself.

"John, I'll break your leg if you don't tell."

"Alright," I said, pointing to the valley. "What is the story of the foot bar on the cross?"

"It wasn't used. He was nailed on the upright," said Arty.

"Yes. Yes. But why is it crooked?"

All I received in reply were blank stares.

"Arty, I'm ashamed of you. You should know. The criminals of course!" More stares. "The criminals who were crucified with Christ." I looked at three blank faces.

"And.." said Arty.

"In the Orthodox Church the footboard is turned up on one side, pointing to the criminal who was saved and promised a place in Heaven. And what does the map say? A 'Sacred Trust'. A sacred promise by Christ to the criminal. That's where the treasure lies. At the point of the upward footboard!"

Chapter 15

"You're joking, surely," grimaced Sutter.

"I'm not and get saddled," I ordered. "We've wasted three days already."

"Might as well, Sturt," shrugged Arty. "He may just be right."

In a few moments, I was back up on Emmett and we were headed back down into the valley. It seemed like only moments to reach the valley floor. Here I reigned up to await the others. It was only a few minutes and they were there with me. We started our search of the finger of hills turning to the northwest, in an orderly fashion. Forming a right oblique with our four horses, Murray still leading our mule, and spaced about 50 yards apart, we moved ahead at a walk, searching the hillsides for some sign of our goal.

We had gone about a mile and a half when our progress was stopped by the precipitate rock of the valley wall. My three companions were perceptibly disheartened. We followed the same system back to our starting point and found no cross or other marker.

"Well. Watson. So much for that theory. What else does your good catholic upbringing say we should try?" came the disheartened words of Sutter.

"She'd say try the other side of the hill. That's what she'd say," I retorted.

Sutter laughed and at least for the moment the tension was broken. So, riding around to the north face, we repeated our process. We had gone perhaps a mile when Arty called out for us to stop.

"Up there," he pointed. "By the large boulder, a cross!"

Rushing to his side, we looked where he pointed. There it was, an orthodox cross, perhaps 100 yards up the side of the rocky finger.

"Murray!" I shouted. "Watch the horses. Come on boys!"

But in the time it took me to say those words, Sutter and Arty were ten yards ahead of me, having leaped off their horses and scrambled forward.

When we reached the large rock with the cross chiselled into it, I started looking about the whole area as the other two began to grab up rocks at its base and look under them like they ere looking for prizes in a Christmas pudding.

"Stop, Gentleman. Stop," I called. The two of them looked at me quizzically. "Let's think this out for a moment. What do we see around the marker and where would you logically think a casket of jewels would be placed?"

The three of us studied the site. "Over here," said Sutter, pointing to a spot to the right of the marker. "The stones appear to be placed and not random. What do you think?"

"I say we move them," was Arty's reply. So pulling up rocks, we removed several layers when we came to a large, flat stone. This stone also had a cross chiselled into it.

"Murray!" I called. "Bring up the pick." In a moment he was with us, and using the pick for a pry bar, we moved the large, flat stone beneath which there was an opening to a cave. The opening was barely large enough for a man of medium build to slide though on his belly. It was but a moment and Sutter had entered the opening, Arty upon his heels, literally. As I prepared to enter, Sutter called back.

"Too dark in here, John. This cave opens up but goes back a considerable distance. We'll need a lantern."

Murray ran back down the hill and was back shortly with our lantern. Lighting the lantern, I passed it to Arty who had crawled back to receive it, and I then followed him in, leaving Murray with instructions to guard the opening.

In the cave, the lantern gave a feeble light, but enough to see by. The cavern extended but about 50 feet and barely tall enough to stand erect in. It was perhaps ten feet wide.

At first the cavern appeared completely empty and we started to search the walls and floors for any sign.

"It can't be gone," moaned Sutter.

"Keep looking," I encouraged.

We continued looking for a few moments when I heard a rush of outgoing air and softly Arty said, "I have it."

There in the far corner where Arty stood with the lantern, just below eye level, was a shelf of rock. We gathered around him and saw an icon, perhaps 4 inches wide by six inches tall, of whom I did not know. But below the icon and sitting directly on the shelf of rock was a small casket of wood, perhaps 8 inches long by 6 inches wide and 4 inches high.

We stood, without touching, and stared at the box. On the lid was some type of oriental scene which somehow seemed incongruous to a holy treasure. Around the edged of the box ran a ribbon of gold inlay and in what appeared to be the eyes of a dragon set two diamonds, each perhaps a carat in size.

"By God," whispered Sutter. "It is real." Reaching forward, he picked up the box and looked it over. "How does it open? I don't see a hinge."

"Try sliding the top," I suggested.

Pressing his thumb down on the lid, it slid easily to one side, exposing the contents. I had never seen so many rubies and diamonds in my life! It was an amazing sight! No settings. No gold. No semi-precious stones. Just diamonds and rubies. It was indeed a fortune.

"Let's get out of here," said Arty. "I want to see it in the daylight."

Picking up the icon, I placed it in my pocket and the three of us headed for the opening. Arty scrambled out first, Sutter behind and I trailed with the lantern.

Sutter had barely entered the opening when I heard Arty calling, "John! John! Get out here quick! Murray's been injured!"

Pushing the lantern in front of me, I scrambled out into the daylight. There, just down the hillside knelt Arty and Sutter looking at the prostrate form of Murray. Rushing over, I saw that I did not need a medical degree to know what happened. He had been struck in the head with something. Blood covered his red hair. Checking his pulse and eyes, I relaxed a bit. Murray would be alright. But surely he hadn't fallen? Then how...

"He has a bally hard head you know."

Turning my head from where I knelt next to Murray, I saw the grinning face of Lieutenant Godard, and in his right hand, was his service revolver, pointed at us.

"He really should have paid more attention to his surroundings, you know. But he was so intent looking in the hole, he never noticed me."

"You Bastard!" I cried.

"Doctor. Doctor. Really, such a temper. I had no idea! Is that my treasure Sturt?" he said, pointing at the box with his revolver.

"You do know you're outnumbered here Godard, don't you?" said Sutter.

"But I'm the one with the gun, old boy. Now just put the box down and all three of you back away."

Sutter hesitated. "Put it down," I said. "He does have the gun."

Sutter looked at me, then back at Godard.

"Follow the Doctor's good advice, Sturt. That's a good man."

Sturt put the box on the ground next to Murray's prostrate form and took a step back.

"Keep going. Back up."

We took three or fours steps down the hill and Godard came forward and stood next to Murray. Keeping the revolver pointed toward us, he reached down and picked up the box.

"Nice of you to find this for me and the Colonel" he sneered. "We'll enjoy it. Maybe I'll even get Violet back. What say, Arty?" The smile was the kind of evil that makes the blood boil.

"Now if you Gentlemen will step over the hill, I'll take my leave." He flicked the revolver toward his left and we moved to our right, allowing him to pass us and go down the hill towards the horses.

Godard was watching us as he stepped forward. It was at that moment I saw Murray's arm shoot forward and seize Godard by the ankle and twist.

Godard fell forward and as he did the revolver fired and I heard Arty scream and go down. Godard scrambled to his feet, the box no longer his. Sturt had pulled his own revolver and fired at Godard, missing as Godard was scrambling, half rolling down the hillside, knowing his only purpose now was escape. Sutter was after him, firing in a fury, but each time he stopped to fire, Godard made progress in his escape, increasing the distance between them.I was busy with Arty. He had been hit in the right upper thigh and was in agony. The large calibre of the bullet had ripped a hole the size of a cricket ball out of his leg as it exited.

Murray was moving now. "Murray, help keep pressure on this. I've got to get my bag." Placing my kerchief on the wound, I placed Murray's hands front and back and ran for the horses. Godard and Sturt disappeared, along with their horses, but for now, I had no time to look for them.

Returning to Arty, I gave him a dose of laudanum and washed and packed the wound as best I could. In fact, he had been fortunate indeed. The bullet not only had passed through, it had hit no bone.

It was fully a half hour before Sturt returned. By then, I had cleaned and bandaged Murray's wound and I had been able to move Arty to the base of the hill. We were busy trying to construct a travois using the cargo tarp from the mule pack when Sturt rode back to us.

"How's Arty?" he asked, stepping down from his horse.

"I'm still alive if that's what you mean," replied Arty. "Where's the bastard?"

"Dead or dying, I think,"

"You think?"

"Brought down his horse about a mile back. He went down with it but got up and made it for the rocks. I followed him for a ways. Pretty sure I hit him at least twice. He made it over the top of the rocks. I decided not to follow our lion cub any further. If he doesn't die of his wounds, maybe the Mohmands will get him. Either way, he's not our problem. Our problem is getting out of here."

We relieved the mule of all the equipment, which we piled in the dust. We filled our water bottles and loaded grain and rations on Arty's horse. The mule would pull the travois with the sticks crossing the pack saddle.

It was now the early afternoon and we decided we would head for the second cross with the hope that Arty's four sowars were still there. We felt we would be able to make it by dark. As we were about to depart, I gave Arty another dose of laudanum. I knew the trip would constitute agony I would not like to suffer.

We progressed well but slowly. As we passed the spot where Godard's horse had gone down, I scanned the hillside for any sign of him. The flies were already gathering on the carcass of the horse. Murray and I continued on as Sturt stopped to search Godard's saddle bags. He re-joined us quickly having found nothing of import. We rode for a while before I spoke.

"What were you expecting to find?" I asked.

"Something to prove Enderby was behind this, but there was nothing there, just kit."

"How do we explain all this, Sutter?"

"We don't, old boy. Godard was just a babe lost in the woods for all we know."

"I had fairly assumed that," I replied. "But I was thinking of Arty."

"Oh, easy enough. Jizail bullet from the hillside. No one will even blink at that. It's Enderby who'll be the problem. When his boy fails to reappear, he will be all over us. He's going to have to come up with some story about Godard's disappearance. We'll just have to take it as it comes." We rode the rest of the way that evening in silence.

We reached the second cross as the last rays of the sun were setting over the western hills. Arty's four sowars were still there, faithfully awaiting their lieutenant's return. Upon seeing their officer on the litter, they rushed to his aid and it was only with the greatest difficulty that I was able to care for and redress his wound due to their constant "assistance".

That evening we took a calculated risk and made a small fire to enable us to make a decent meal for our invalid. Arty's daffadar quickly organized the three sowars and assigned them to various duties of attending their lieutenant and standing guard on the hillsides. Murray had attended to our animals while I was occupied with my duties at Arty's side. Later, while the sowars stood guard and Arty slept, Sutter, Murray and I sat near the campfire.

"Excuse me, Sir," said Murray. "Hadn't we best put this out? I can fill it in."

"Yes, I suppose so," I agreed. "No use taking unnecessary risks."

"Before you do," chimed in Sturt, "I want to tell you both what I've done. While you both were occupied tonight, I reburied the box."

"You what?" I exclaimed.

"Yes, I know. We've gone through all this to find it but I have a bad feeling about it. It's where any of us can find it. It's covered by rock at the base of the cross up by the trail. I have no fear it will be found and we can come back for it now that we know where it is. We're going to have enough to explain at the moment and Enderby is going to be very curious about his missing dog."

I thought about this for a moment and, looking at Murray, nodded to him.

"It makes sense to me. At least we know where it is. What you say, Murray?"

"Yes, Sir. As you say, we best come back later."

Having agreed to this, Murray started to cover the fire and I went in search of some sleep. Fortunately sleep came quickly and the next I was aware; Sutter was shaking me awake as the first rays of false dawn could be seen.

I rose and tended to Arty, who was now showing signs of a low grade fever. That was to be expected of course. In the meantime, Murray and the daffadar had been seeing to saddling and packing. I had just finished with Arty and was wanting my bit of dried beef and new potato when the sowar who had been posted on the hillside raced into camp. He reported straight to the daffadar. I knew something was wrong. The two came quickly to where Sturt stood by the cold fire pit, said something and then turned and went to gather their horses from the line.

"Doctor! Private Murray!" called Sturt. "Quick as you can now! Horses! There are a dozen or so Mohmands trying to circle us from the north! We've got to move now! Quick as you can!"

Fortunately we were prepared to move except that we hadn't set Arty on the travois yet. Murray brought up our mule and with the help of one of the sowars, I placed him on it. We tied a lead strap under his arms, attaching it to the travois lest he should slide down and off. We had no time for the slow movement of the day before. Speed was essential if we were to escape.

Our preparations took but moments and we were up on the trail moving at a brisk walk. The daffadar and one sowar took the lead, then I leading one mule and Murray the second, which transported Arty. Sturt and the other two sowars brought up the rear of our little column.

Within minutes I could see the turbans on hillsides as they raced to try and get ahead of us. I knew it was at least six miles to the main Dakka-Jalalabad road. The entire trail could now turn into a deadly gauntlet from which we might not reappear.

I could now hear firing to our rear. We were keeping a good pace and I knew that the men moving along the hilltops could not keep up. If we could keep the Mohmands from overtaking us by the trail, we should prove to be alright. My one worry was that "lucky" shot from a hillside.

By the time we reached the first cross, we had outstripped those on the hills but now Sutter and his sowars were no longer even occasionally in sight and the sounds of firing increased.

We had halved the distance to the road again when one of the sowars rushed past me up to the daffadar. The daffadar and both sowars turned their horses about and as they rushed past, the daffadar reigned up for a moment.

"Sir. Please to continue. We shall return."

With that, he was gone after his men. I continued and for a few moments I could hear a great increase in rifle fire.

Within 15 minutes, we were out upon the road and I slackened the pace. Another mile and I stopped to check on Arty. His wound had reopened and I could see the agony in his face.

"Don't worry about it, John" he smiled. "I'm going to be fine. Let's keep moving. We're not safe yet."

"Two hours and we'll be in Dakka," I told him. "but first, I'm going to re-bind your wound. Then we'll move on."

I quickly rebound the wound and we moved off again. It now seemed that our luck had changed for we met a patrol of Bengal Cavalry by a Jemadar.

I quickly explained that Lieutenant Sturt and four men had been holding off the attack of the Mohmands to allow our escape. Leaving four men to escort us to Dakka, he galloped off with the rest of his patrol to extricate our little force. So it was that about two hours later, with great relief, we entered the fort at Dakka.

The next hour was busy. I installed Arty in the hospital and was now able to properly treat him. The Surgeon Major agreed that after a day's rest, Arty would be sent to the hospital at Peshawar.

Having taken care of the animals, Murray came to find me. We had had no word about Sturt nor of the patrol which had gone to his aid. It was not until the late afternoon that the patrol returned. It was the Jemadar who had led the patrol who came to find me at the hospital. Two of his men had been wounded slightly and were being brought in. But the worst news was yet to come. There had been one fatality, Lieutenant Sutter Sturt, of the 5th Regiment of Foot.

Chapter 16

I was stunned. This could not be! Sturt, dead? I had to go somewhere and think. Other people died, not my friends. And his treasure, for I thought of it as his, he'd had such plans. Plans weren't much use now. The sadness overwhelmed me.

I decided not to talk to Arty about it until the next evening. By then, he would be wondering at not having seen our friend, but for now, he needed rest.

In the meantime, I was called to the headquarters and asked to report what had happened. I kept to the story that Suttor had proposed. No sightings of gatherings of Mohmands until McMullen had been hit by a surprise sniper. The rest was easy, I merely made no mention of treasure or Lieutenant Godard and gave the details of our escape the day following Arty's wounding. It was all taken at face value and I was allowed to return to the hospital.

That night, I broke the news to Arty. He appeared to have no reaction. He stared off into the ceiling for a while.

"I think I need some rest, John. Do you mind?"

"No, but if you decide to, we can talk tomorrow before your convoy leaves for Peshawar."

"Yes, we'll talk then. Good Night, John." With that, he closed his eyes and I left.

I didn't sleep that night. All our adventures kept flooding my thoughts. One gets very hardened to death and suffering of others in the Army. But when it's your own, well, that's different. I never have gotten over Sturt's death. Come the morning, I went to see Arty prior to the convoy's departure.

"Sorry you won't be here for the funeral," I said. "But you need to get to Peshawar as soon as possible. Best hospital we have you know."

"Oh, I'll be fine, John. Be back in the saddle in no time. As for funerals, well, I've seen plenty of them. Sutter wouldn't want us moping about. He did his job, what else needs to be said? I'll surely miss him though. I do have something else to say," he looked about to make sure we were alone. "I don't want my share of the treasure, John. Do what you want with it. You already know my feelings."

"Arty, surely you need to give this time, think it over."

"I have John, all night. Don't worry about me regretting it. I won't. Understand?"

As they loaded Arty into the ambulance, I said goodbye and shook his hand. We would meet again, sooner than I expected.

That afternoon we buried Sturt in the cemetery under the walls of the fort. Reverence for the dead and the conduct of the funeral is something the Army does well.

We paraded for funeral at half one and all were in dress uniform. The garrison paraded at the slow march, rifles reversed, to the cemetery. It was indeed a solemn procession. Sturt would have appreciated it. I couldn't help smiling thinking that somewhere, Sturt was also smiling. I resisted the temptation to bless myself at the end of the chaplain's words and as the soldiers marched off the band, played a cheery little dance hall ditty. How odd, I thought.

As I walked back to the hospital, I wondered what to do next. It was now the 5th of June. The convoy of cannon was due tomorrow. I reasoned the best thing to do would be move on with the convoy on the 7th,. Go on back to Jalalabad. So we did.

Murray and I arrived at Jalalabad on the 9th. Colour Sergeant Wood had commanded the company on the return trip. Arty's havaldar had taken his detachment to Peshawar in concert with the convoy moving their Lieutenant. I don't know that they had orders to do so but no one thought to question them.

I was in a sad mood at Jalalabad. The line officers seemed to deal with losses differently than I did. Among them there was a much more fatalistic attitude. It was not that they did not care about their fellow officer. In fact, he would be remembered on the role of "honoured dead". It was more than that; this was the business they were in. Death was common enough in peace, in active service, it was an expectation. So while the officer's mess that night had a certain sombreness to it, (there were many questions) there was also a light heartedness. Hurrah for Sturt, may his soul stand guard in the streets of Heaven.

I went about my duties that first day back with little to say to anyone. I was able to wire through to Peshawar and found that Arty was doing well and should be returned to duty in a month or two. He also had kept with our arranged story, a sniper from the hills.

It was on our first day back in Jalalabad that I was sent for by Major Tucker. I reported at the headquarters.

"Doctor. Good of you to come so quickly. I've been instructed to ask you some questions about the incident in which Lieutenant Sturt was killed."

"Gladly, Sir, but I don't know what I can really tell you since I did not actually see what happened. I and my orderly were taking Lieutenant McMullen to safety. Perhaps the Jemadar from the 12th Bengal saw something."

"I understand that McMullen was wounded in the incident. Not seriously, I hope."

"Serious enough. Should be back to duty in a month or so. But to answer your questions, no. He was wounded the day before." At this point I detailed the story as Murray and I had rehearsed it. Everything was exactly as it happened except there was no treasure and Godard was never mentioned.

When I had finished, Tucker leaned back in his chair behind the desk and looked at me for a moment. "You know, Doctor, that almost word for word, what your orderly told me. I wonder why?"

"Perhaps because it was what happened. And of course, we have discussed it at great length, trying to decide what we might have done differently."

"Well, that does seem to make a certain amount of sense." He now leaned forward over the desk and looked at me intently. "I've received a wire from Colonel Enderby of the General Staff. He's asking about Lieutenant Godard and seems to think you might know where he is."

I furrowed my brow and thought a moment. Did I know where Godard was? In truth, I didn't. Sturt had said he'd wounded him, but where he went in his run from Sturt or where he was now, I had no idea.

"No, Sir. I cannot say that I know. Is he on leave?"

"Yes, he took a week but why should Colonel Enderby think you would know?"

"I'm sure I can't say, Sir. Is that all?" I rose from my chair.

"That's all, Doctor," he said, rising also. Coming around the desk, he patted my shoulder. "Sorry about Sturt. I know you and he were great friends. Well, carry on."

I left with a feeling of dread. I was now in a position I had never imagined I would be in. And I had placed Murray in a like position. We had found the treasure, yes, but we were now lying about the whole incident. If only Godard hadn't tried to steal the treasure, if he hadn't shot Arty, if Sturt hadn't shot Godard. What a mess had become of such a great adventure. I sought Murray out and asked him about his interview with Major Tucker. True to Tucker's statement, the stories had been consistent. But our troubles were not yet over.

That evening, I received orders to report to the hospital at Peshawar and Murray was ordered with me. We started the following morning. I knew who had arranged this, for who would want to talk to me at Peshawar? Only Enderby.

It was the 12th of June before we arrived at Peshawar and my first act was to go see Arty. He was still assigned to the hospital but the wound was healing well and as long as he didn't overextend, he could get about. I met him outside where he sat in a gazebo, shaded from the afternoon sun.

"Watson!" he cried as I entered and started to stand.

"Sit down you fool or I'll be in trouble for re-opening your wound," I grinned.

"Excellent to see you!" He settled back in his wicker chair. "But let me guess what brings you here." He grinned from ear to ear. "You've been ordered to Peshawar and you're going to get a call to visit our friend the Colonel, eh?"

"That about has it." I said, sitting in the chair next to him.

"Yes, well, old boy tried to bully me about it, didn't do him any good. Didn't see Godard, don't know anything about a treasure. Held his little palaver in private so he didn't have to say the word 'treasure' in front of anyone else. Poor soul is beside himself with rage. He doesn't know if we did something to Godard or if Godard has double-crossed him. He's in quite a tizzy.

"Tell me, Arty. What do we do about the treasure?"

He took a long breath and sighed. "I've told you, John. I don't want any of it. I just want to get back to the 18th and get on with it. It's all yours and Murray's for all I care. Queen's regulations say if we find a treasure, we're supposed to turn it to the crown. We would be entitled to a 10 per cent share."

"Sturt never told me that."

"Lots of things Sturt didn't tell." Arty was quiet a moment. "I really miss him."

We sat quietly for a while.

"I'd best report in." I finally said, getting to my feet. "I'll check back in on you soon."

That evening I was summoned to General Headquarters to report to Colonel Enderby. My loathing of the man was reaching no bounds. I entered the headquarters and found it almost deserted. A sergeant at the front desk asked if he might help me.

"I'm to report to Colonel Enderby."

"Ah, yes, Sir. Second door right, Sir."

"Thank you, Sergeant." I answered. Turning, I went to the door indicated and finding it closed, I knocked.

"Enter." It was Enderby's voice.

Entering, I took the scene in quickly. Enderby was alone in the small room. There was only a small table and two chairs and behind where the Colonel sat, a window, closed even though the heat was oppressive. This was to be a private discussion indeed.

Enderby was watching me intently as I closed the door. I then reported and stood at attention waiting. For a moment, he said nothing. He looked me up and down as if considering his course of action. Finally, he made a decision.

"Have a chair, Doctor. We know each other fairly well, no standing on formality.

"Well, Sir, I do have a number of patients to attend to. Is there something I can do for you?" I stood where I was, not moving toward the chair as proffered.

"First, Doctor, I want you to know that whatever our differences, I'm still sorry about your friends."

"Thank You, Sir. But what is it I can do for you?"

"Alright, Watson, have it your way. What were you and Sturt doing out near Dakka and where is Godard? That's that I want to know." He leaned forward over the table, his face was tinged with red and his breathing was coming quickly.

"It was a reconnaissance patrol and I don't know where Godard is," I replied.

"Bull!" he yelled, slamming his fist on the table. "You were looking for the treasure! Do you think I'm a fool?"

I stood my ground and looked at him with a smile.

"Do you really believe you can fight me, Doctor?" His control was returning. "What have you done to Godard?"

"Sir, I assure you that I have done nothing to Godard. Is he lost?"

"You know damn well he is missing. If I can prove you or the other two have done him in, even the treasure won't save you. Do I make myself clear?"

"Quite, Sir. Anything else?"

"Yes, I believe your services are going to be needed around Kandahar. I've arranged with the medical department to have you reassigned down there. You'll be taking Private Murray with you. The two of you can perhaps remember better what happened last week."

Saluting, I turned about and left the room. Kandahar was as far away in Afghanistan as he could send me. Perhaps it would be a good thing.

Chapter 17

It was Friday, the 12th of June when Murray and I left for Kandahar. We were being sent to the 66th Regiment of Foot. An outstanding regiment with a great history and just recently arrived in Afghanistan.

In my writings over the years, I had mentioned that I was "removed" from my regiment. Those not truly familiar with the Army system assumed I meant seconded. They were wrong for two reasons. Firstly, at that time, medical officers were not properly part of a regiment. They belonged to the Medical Department and assigned as needed. Secondly, I felt "removed". I was disposed of by a loathsome creature, to better his own position, but the result of these actions would lead me to a wonderful place in the end. It would lead me to Baker Street. Miss Eileen had always been right. God, indeed, has plans.

It took about a week on the military road to travel the distance from Peshawar to Jhelum. Before we left, I had visited Arty one last time. We wished each other well and I never saw him again. I did keep up with his career and saw he was mentioned in dispatch from the Kurram Valley. We have corresponded over the years.

On arriving at Jhelum, I was fortunate to get room on the transport train for Emmett as I was loath to part with such a good horse. I felt in a way fortunate to be on my way to the 66th. Things had been relatively quiet in the Khyber and the fighting appeared to be moving south. Ayub Khan had not been installed by the British government but instead Abdul Rahman was to be given the throne. Ayub Khan was gathering forces outside Herat and I would be needed. The treasure and other troubles were pushed from my mind.

Four days later, Murray and I arrived at Sibi, the northern terminus of rail leading toward Kandahar. It had not existed the last time I had passed the area. Colonel Lindsay, R.E. had been given the task to complete the line from RUK junction to Sibi, a distance of 133 miles, in order to eliminate the requirement to walk across a horrible desert. He accomplished this at the rate of one mile a day with almost no injury to the men. A truly remarkable effort. The survey was now in hand to extend the line to Quetta.

At Sibi, I was able once again to secure a mount for Murray. We were traveling with a few impediments as most our kit was still in Jalalabad. Even so, it would take 10 days to reach Kandahar and during our journey, there were forces moving of which we, nor the British, had any knowledge.

Much is known now about what was happening, but at the time, British intelligence had completely failed. Spies were caught, reconnaissance was poor and deciphering of what intelligence there was, was left to political officers. The countryside from Sibi to Kandahar was deceptively quite, but as Murray and I moved toward the 66th, Sadar Mohammed Ayub Khan was also moving toward Kandahar, along with 20,000 soldiers and 30 cannon. His location and exact strength were completely unknown to General Primrose and the British Army.

As Murray and I proceeded in the false calm, Ayub Khan was moving his cavalry from Herat. As we had ridden the train, the Wali of Kandahar was at Girishk asking for British troops to support his soldiers, who were wavering on the verge of going over to Ayub Khan. As Ayub Khan approached Girishk, he was gathering tribes along the way and moved slowly in order for the gathering to occur. He had even succeeded in quelling some of the squabbling between the Kabuli and Herati. Ayub had succeeded in getting to Farah before Primrose had even received permission to support the Wali. Massive troop movements from India would be required to support Primrose. None of this did two lowly soldiers know, as we walked our horses towards Kandahar.

It was late on the 3rd of July when we arrived at Kandahar cantonment. Unbeknownst to me, I had only 4 weeks left to my active Army career.

Having reported in at the 66h to Major C.F. Oliver, I was given into the care of their Surgeon Major, A.F. Preston, with an admonition to return later to meet Colonel Galbraith.

"Well, Doctor, we're very pleased to have you along. We've just learned this morning that we march in two days for Girishk. Much to do, much to do."

We talked as we went from the headquarters building toward the hospital area.

"We can much use some more help, hard pressed for help. At least anyone that knows anything. Come from Peshawar, have you?"

147

I wondered if he knew why I was there but decided not to raise the subject. He was a fine gentleman from his looks and speech. He was probably 5 foot 8 or 9, greying hair and moustache and a pleasant smile. His skin was tanned and wrinkled from many years in the orient and I knew he had a reputation as a good doctor and caring soldier.

"Yes, Surgeon Major. Been here a while now, but what is it that you would like me to do?"

"We'll get you properly started tomorrow first thing, but what I need most right now is for you to meet our staff and then get some rest. Had anything to eat?"

"I must admit not since early this morning."

"Excellent. Excellent. So, first to the mess, I'm sure your man can take care of your kit. I'll have my man see that he's well taken care of."

"And the duty tomorrow?" I asked.

"Need you to start going through the people the Commissary boys are sending us." He stopped walking for a moment and clasping his hands behind his back and looked me straight in the eyes. "As you know, we don't hire our own men. Damnable shame I call it! Commissary Department goes about the streets hiring riff raff and fools to be dressers or compounders or ward servants or doolie bearers or whatever. We in the medical department must be allowed to train and hire our own! Damnable, that's what I say!" With that he grinned and took a deep breath. "Right then. Excellent. Excellent. How about something to eat?"

I laughed and we went off to meet and eat.

The next morning was a frantic scene. The cavalry brigade under Brigadier General Nuttall left Kandahar with the 3rd Sind Horse and 3rd Bombay Light Cavalry. The Infantry Brigade with the 66th Foot, 1st Grenadiers, Bombay Infantry and Jacob's Rifles along with E-B of the Royal Horse Artillery, No. 2 Company Sappers and Miners, Commissariat, Hospital and ordnance stores would follow the next day.

I watched with great interest as the months of supply, rations and equipment to support 2800 men was loaded on wagons, camels and mules. For awhile, there were over 2400 soldiers to be fed and cared for, there were the muleteers, camel drivers, doolie bearers, etc., who also must eat. Add to this, grain and bhusa for the 3000 animals and the convoy would stretch for miles. But against what appeared to be a sizable force were to be arrayed perhaps 15,000 Afghanis, as many as four regiments of regulars from Kabul plus more from Herat. Much would depend on the allegiance of the Wali's 4000 men.

It was barely light on the 5th when we marched out. Once again, my position gave me great freedom of movement. While Murray stayed with the hospital near the front of the baggage column, I roved from place to place, asking questions of our situation. It was at this point I met Captain Slade of the Royal Horse Artillery.

Captain Slade had been detailed to General Burrow's staff as an orderly officer. This really was a position of trust as his duty was to gallop orders to different parts of the field of battle. It takes someone knowledgeable of military affairs to properly communicate oral orders and have them understood. In later years, he would be British Commander in Egypt.

I had ridden up alongside him as he was keeping just to the rear of the staff. "Good morning, Captain." I said and saluted.

Looking over his shoulder, he returned the salute. "Good Morning, Surgeon. Hope there's no problem."

"No Sir. Just inquisitive. Like to know what's happening so I can be prepared."

He looked me up and down for a moment as if considering if I were serious or a fool. He finally nodded as though he made a decision and smiled through his moustache. "Good idea to know what's happening. Lets one plan for contingencies. What regiment are you with, Doctor? I don't remember seeing you before."

I introduced myself and explained I had just arrived from the Khyber Field Force.

"Well, you should have seen a bit then. Our job is going to be to keep old Ayub Khan from trying to take Kandahar. We've support coming from India but he'll be here before they will. Or so we think. The Wali has just been installed and we're none too sure of his followers. Our job is to make his men stand and fight with us if Ayub Khan actually comes."

"I must admit, I've no faith in the Afghans ever taking one side or the other. It seems to be expediency of the moment with them."

He looked at me for another moment and then came a great guffaw. "By God, Doctor, you do understand these people!"

We continued to ride together and spoke at length of our situation. If the Wali's men stood fast, a good defensive position could be established and even at a disadvantage of two to one or three to one, we were sure of holding.

We had been talking the better part of an hour when I decided that I had been gone long enough from my position and took my leave. The Captain had impressed me. He appeared to have an excellent understanding of our situation and capabilities. He was also a superb horseman, as were most horse artillerymen.

That night, having travelled but seven miles, we camped at Kohkaran and I went about the normal business of blisters and boils. Each day, for seven days, we made camp where the cavalry brigade had camped the night before. This system was necessitated by the large number of animals each brigade had and the limited grazing available.

I saw Captain Slade a few times over the following week but spent some of my time getting to know the officers of the 66th. Colonel Galbraith and all his officers were excellent men. Most of my time, however, we spent at the end of the day's march trying to explain the duties required of the newly hired natives to them with the help of those who had been there. We made adequate progress under trying conditions. For after a day's march, camp must be set, animals cared for, defences built and men fed. There was little time for instruction. Through it all, Surgeon Major Preston was a steady friend, helping to guide me through my additional duties.

During the march itself, I made it a point to get about and meet each of the officers of the 66th. Captains Cullen and Roberts were especially friendly and made it a point to seek me out each night as did Lieutenant Faunce. All of whom were great horse fanciers and we spent a bit of time talking about the merits of different horses and jockeys.

On the fourth night, we reached Kushk-i-Nakhud. (We would return here sooner than we had expected.) And by the 11th of July we arrived at the Helmand River directly across from the Wali's fort at Girishk.

Chapter 18

On the day of our arrival at the Helmand River, we were still unaware of Ayub Khan's nearness. His cavalry was already at Washir. We were not in a good location nor was luck with us at the moment. General Burrows had been ordered by General Primrose not to cross the Helmand but the Wali's fort of Girishk was on the opposite bank, forcing us to form a defensive position separate from the Wali.

The last leg of our journey had only been six miles and as the infantry worked on establishing our defensive perimeter Surgeon Major Preston, Surgeon Collins and I strove to establish a working hospital in concert with the Surgeons of the other regiments.

Late that evening, I ventured over to where the 66th had established its headquarters to see what information I could glean from the officers. I wanted to know how long we would be in place and if there was word of our enemy for our camp was an open plain with little cover. I found Major Oliver standing by a campfire, smoking a pipe and looking very introspective.

"Good Evening, Sir. Mind some company?"

He looked at me a second as if gathering his thoughts. "No, Doctor. By all means. All going well at hospital? No list of illness to report, I hope."

"No, Sir. The soldiers are in quite good shape. Normal problems." I took out my pipe and as I started to change the bowl, the Major turned back toward the fire.

"Any idea how long we'll be in this position, Sir?" I asked. "Just want to know for planning purposes. How much to get off the wagons, etc. You know the issues."

The Major thought for a moment as if deciding what to say. He looked around and seeing we were alone, moved closer to me.

"Look, Doctor" he said sotto voce. "This place we're in is a great parade ground but it can't be defended. We're not allowed to cross the river, which would be the best thing. It's easily fordable this time of year. We either need to move across the river or find another spot. See that wooded area just across the river?" He pointed and I turned and looked. "Put a few cannon in there and some good riflemen and they would give us a beating out here in the open." He turned back and smoked for a moment more. "No, Doctor, don't put too much on the ground. We will need to move."

We smoked for a few more moments and then I took my leave. Major Oliver was still studying the fire as I left.

The next few days were spent quietly while the troops tried to improve our position. I talked with Captain Slade the following morning and learned that most of the Wali's troops were in a mutinous mood. A number that reached 6000. One of the Wali's sardars had already deserted with the Alizais but for the moment, the rest of the soldiers remained.

We had been four days on our "parade field" and were finally given the order to move further up the river to a more defensible position when the worst news possible came. The Wali's soldiers had deserted en-masse and were headed to join Ayub Khan who was now reported only 55 miles away at Eklang, or at least his cavalry was there. The Wali's force deserted well armed, taking 6 cannon and massive amounts of small arms and ammunition.

Oddly, the Wali's cavalry took it upon themselves to deliver the Wali and his treasure to our political officer, Lieutenant Colonel St. John, before deserting themselves. What was even more unusual was that instead of going toward Ayub's cavalry, they headed towards Kandahar as if to wait for Ayub Khan to catch up.

Murray ran into the hospital area as we were tearing down to load the wagons.

"Sir, General Burrows has ordered a column to chase the Wali's forces and disperse them and reclaim the cannon. The 66th is sending 4 companies. Do we go?"

"I say yes, but we'll have to get permission from the Surgeon Major. Start packing two mules and I'll be right back." So saying, I went in search of permission. It was easily obtained. By the time I returned, Murray had two mules packed, a handful of doolie bearers and Emmett saddled. As the 66th moved off in pursuit, we trailed the column.

Besides the 66th Foot, there were three companies of Jacob's Rifles and the No. 2 Company of Sappers and Miners. In the distance, I could see the elements of the 3rd Sind Horse and 3rd Bombay Cavalry, along with our battery of Horse Artillery. The mounted units quickly outdistanced us and by the time we reached the ford of the Helmand, two miles distant, they were but a dust cloud. It was now mid-morning.

As we struggled on in the heat, it was the duty of the infantry to clear a number of villages and nalas to the right of our line of march. The mounted units were little impeded by the few Afghans who sniped at them along the way. The infantry, moving more slowly, came under more constant fire. More importantly, we did not know their strength and therefore, whether they posed a clear threat. Each village and gully had to be cleared as we marched. By noon, I had two wounded and before the day was over, two more. One would die in August of the wounds he suffered, Private John Holmes.

By 11 o'clock, we could hear distant small arms fire. The cavalry under General Nuttall was trying to hold the enemy in place while they awaited the cannons and Infantry. In a few moments, we could hear the cannon fire. But it was not the crack of rifled guns; it was the ring of smooth bores. The rebels had opened up with their cannon on our cavalry. The officers started pushing our soldiers to move more quickly. I bandaged an arm as I walked beside our mules, pressing forward.

Now came the crack-thump of the rifled guns. The Royal Horse was in the fight. As we marched, the cannons played point and counter-point. Gradually, the ringing of smooth bores came less and less frequently. Major Blackwood's battery was winning through! The cannons had been duelling for more than half an hour.

As we crested a hill, I could see the bulk of the cavalry riding to the left. They were going to take the battery which the mutineers had abandoned. There were, however, enough of the enemy infantry to cause the cavalry to dismount and fight as skirmishers. The Royal Horse was moving forward also and in a few moments they were in action again, throwing shell among the Afghans and causing them to flee once more.

Our cavalry mounted and gave chase until the hillsides prevented further pursuit. We were now in possession of their artillery, their ammunition and their supplies. By 4 pm., we had returned to camp, the 66th Foot escorting the captured battery with drivers supplied by the Royal Horse.

That night, as I sat on the tail board of the ambulance, cleaning my Webley, Murray approached.

"Excuse me, Sir, but I thought you might want to know there's a big palaver going on at the headquarters."

"I'm sure they'll let us know what's going on, Murray," I said, putting away my rags and oil. "But I haven't had a pipe all day, think I'll see what the Surgeon Major knows.

"Yes, Sir," smiled Murray. "Excellent idea. I believe I'll check water barrels. Evening, Sir." With a knowing nod, he saluted and left.

Re-holstering my revolver, I secured my pipe and helmet and went in search of Dr Preston. He was with Major Oliver at the Major's tent.

"Ah, Doctor Watson. Excellent. Excellent. It looks like we'll be leaving in the morning," grinned Preston.

"No official word yet," interrupted Oliver. "Be the best plan though."

"Why is that, Sir? Is there word of Ayub Khan?" I asked.

"We know his cavalry is at Eklang, about 55 miles from here, and according to Lieutenant Colonel St. John, he's probably got 15,000 men assembled at this point. Let me show you what the problem is." Oliver got up and going to his table, unrolled a map.

"Look, Doctor. We're here, at Girishk on the Kandahar side of the Helmand. Now, our orders are to keep Ayub Khan from marching on Kandahar by making him stay on his side of the river."

"I understand, Sir."

"Well, there are just a few problems with that, good fellow." He pointed at the map again. "The Wali's soldiers, who we were supposed to fight with, have deserted and taken their Snider rifles. His cavalry has just dispersed but his infantry is joining Ayub Khan. That may bring his strength to 20, 000. Now, the river is falling and within a day or two, he won't have to come through here." He stabbed at the paper. "He can cross anywhere. He can cross above or below us. We also have no supplies. We have water and grazing for the moment, but we'd need grain for the animals and food for the men. I believe, we'll be moving back to a more defensible position closer to Kandahar. Right now, we're outnumbered almost ten to one. If I were you, Doctor," he looked me in the eyes, "I'd be checking my bandages."

The next morning, the decision was made to move back to Kushk-i-Nakhud where supplies could be had. There was an old fort there and it sat upon the Girishk-Kandahar road by the Maiwand Pass.

The ponderous task of an Army packing for the move took most of the day and the march didn't start until 7 that night. Before we left, I could see a huge fire down by the river and went to investigate. There, I met Captain Slade. He was in a fury.

"What's going on, Captain?"

"I live among fools, Doctor." He looked at me, hands on his hips and shaking his head. "That heap of charcoal you're looking at is ammunition wagons for the battery we captured yesterday. And those fools," he pointed at the soldiers "are throwing ammunition in the river!"

"But why?" I exclaimed.

"Because there aren't enough horses to go around for cannons and baggage. We've already sent a dispatch to Kandahar asking for more horses but instead of leaving tents and cots, we are leaving ammunition. I tell you, Doctor, they may well regret this." He shook his head again.

Inwardly, I grinned a bit and thought, "An artilleryman's love of his sport". Outwardly, I asked, "What of the guns?"

"Oh, we'll move them, and each gun has 52 rounds with it. I've even convinced Blackwood to haul some of the ammunition for these guns. He believes it's a mistake also." Once again, he shook his head and with a parting look at the burning wagons, turned on his heel and left.

The march the first night was about 26 miles. We arrived at Mis Karez about mid-morning the following day. Men and beasts were exhausted, having been on the march for 14 hours and without sleep for 27. We rested here the rest of the day and started the march again the following day. It was a short march of about 8 miles. We were now 84 miles from Girishk and 46 miles from Kandahar. On this day, Ayub Khan's cavalry entered Girishk. Heliograph messages and dispatch riders were now flowing between Kusk-i-Nakhud and Kandahar. We camped on the Kandahar side of the old fort in what appeared to be a good spot.

Loading and unloading our little hospital had become fairly routine. Our training of the commissary hires had gone well and as a consequence, there was little for me to supervise. I decided to walk through the 66th's camp and talk with the men.

On the whole, all to whom I spoke were in good spirits, but the constant marching was beginning to show. They were willing, but tired, and I made a note to myself to talk to Major Oliver about what we could do to help the situation. As things happen, I was able to speak to him that evening and he assured me that, at least for the moment, General Burrows intended to stay at Kushk-i-Nakhud. As I left the Major's tent, I could see more dispatch riders coming and going from the General's staff tent and wondered what new orders they brought.

Late the next evening, I sat smoking my pipe and found myself wondering how Arty was fairing and where he was. My thoughts were broken by Murray, who came to tell me that we were moving again in the morning. The move was only a distance of three miles to the right bank of the Kushk-i-Nakhud stream. I had come to the point of admitting I did not understand military tactics, for we were moving from what appeared to me a good position from which to fight and 5500 men and over 3000 animals were moving to an open valley. Perhaps it was to position to better intercept Ayub Khan. I just didn't know.

As we unloaded again at our new position, a detachment of 3rd Sind Horse arrived from Kandahar, bringing more horses and more dispatches. As had become my norm, I went in search of information. I could see the men of the 66th digging breastworks, but an officer was walking the ranks, calling out the occasional soldier, who dropped his tools and taking up his rifle and equipment was falling into formation. Thinking that perhaps there was another large patrol, I hurried over to see if my assistance would be required. I found Lieutenant Faunce giving the formation over to a Sergeant to march off.

"Lieutenant Faunce, is there a patrol?"

"Ah, Doctor. No. It seems that Captain Slade has convinced the General to form a provisional battery with the Wali's cannons. I was told to find 42 men who had some knowledge and toll them off to the good Captain. I go also."

"You don't seem displeased," I remarked, for surely he was grinning under the skin.

"Well, chance to do something different, always liked the cannons. He's also pulled Lieutenant Fowle from the Ordnance and Lieutenant Jones from Transport. They're both Royal Artillery. We'll each take two guns and see what we can do. Major Blackwood is sending men to command each piece."

His demeanour changed and looking somewhat more serious, he looked to the hills that surrounded us. "Doctor, if we're attacked here, we'll need every cannon we got. We're surrounded by high ground. I hope they have adequate reconnaissance out."

I gazed around me in a complete circle, while Faunce watched me. He was right, this was a bad location. At no point could you see beyond a mile.

"Well, I saw more cavalry coming in, surely that will help."

"Let's hope, Doctor. They brought more horses for the Wali's battery too. At least we'll have enough artillery horses to move the guns. The Lieutenant who came with them seems a decent fellow, name of Dragon I think, lost an eye in Africa last year. Anyway, must be off to drill the men. See you later, Doctor."

Over the next few days, except in front of the 66th, little improvement was made to our position. The Jacob's Rifles and the 1st built breast works out of the kit bags and camel saddles. Day after day brought no news of Ayub Khan and his horde. The cavalry patrolled constantly but nothing was seen.

I spent a considerable amount of time over at the Wali's battery, watching the 66th's new gunners train. They were quick studies and Captain Slade kept them working until every crew was precise in its drill.

Murray came to me one afternoon to discuss some concerns of the day's orders. Once we had disposed of business, he hesitated.

"What is it, Murray? You've something to say?"

"Well, Sir. All this time since our little incident back at Dakka, you see. And well, I've been thinking. What do we do about the treasure?"

"I've thought about that too, Murray." I put down my pipe and looked at the camp before us. "Doesn't seem too important at the moment."

"No, Sir. That's what I was thinking. Doesn't mean much. At least not out here. I keep thinking about Lieutenant Sturt. He might be here if we hadn't gone looking for it."

"It's what he wanted to do. He'd also be here if Colonel Enderby hadn't sent Godard after us. Godard would be here too."

I turned back to my pipe and started to recharge it. "I believe, Murray, it's better left where it is."

"Thank you, Sir. I'd much the same idea. I'll be getting back now, Sir." He saluted and was off.

That night, Surgeon Major Preston and I decided to visit Major Oliver and try to determine what the forces status was. We had heard that the Bombay Cavalry had a short fight that morning and we wanted to know if a fight was expected. We found him at his tent.

"I'm happy to tell you what I know," Oliver stated, leaning back on his camp stool. "Colonel St. John can only give us the merest estimates. We know the Wali's men, with our rifles mind you, have joined Ayub Khan. St. John thinks we're facing about 5000 infantry, 3000 cavalry, about half regular and half irregulars and 30 cannon. Plus there will be 5 or 6 thousand ghazis armed with who knows what."

"We know they're close, but we don't know where. And our job is still to keep them from attacking Kandahar until it can be reinforced. That little skirmish the cavalry had this morning was against about 500 horse according to Major Leach. They've increased patrols, but unless we can find them, we don't have a plan of attack."

The afternoon of the 25th, Lieutenant Smith of the 3rd Sind Horse, finally brought some positive news. He'd been to Maiwand and found that Ayub's patrols were almost to Sangbar and that Ayub himself would be in Maiwand by Tuesday the 27th. Ghazis were already starting to assemble in Maiwand, awaiting their leader. General Burrows decided to beat Ayub Khan to Maiwand and stop his advance on Kandahar in compliance with his orders. It was a decision that would change my life forever.

Chapter 19

Much has been said and written about the battle of Maiwand. I can only describe it as I knew it. What I saw was not the big picture of tactics and strategies. What I saw was the close in fight of desperate men against overwhelming odds. Did Ayub Khan outnumber our force by 10 to one or only 8 to one? I don't know. Neither does anyone else, not even Ayub Khan himself. That we were to lose 1000 men and Ayub Khan 5000, was hours in the future. We would suffer a severe tactical defeat and yet achieve a strategic victory.

We had started packing at 10:30 on the night of the 26th and the force paraded at 4:30 in the morning. It would be seven before the advance party would leave and in the intervening lull, I tried to eat some dried beef and drink some water. In the Army, at that time, the practice was to have the last meal of the day at four in the afternoon so it had already been a long time since we had eaten and there was to be no morning meal. I was sitting astride Emmett near the hospital wagons as the sun rose, smoking my first pipe of the day, when Captain Slade rode by.

"Morning, Doctor. Ready to march?" he said, reigning up.

"Any time you are, Captain. There will be some action today, I expect."

"Yes, I think there will be. Would you like to ride along with the smooth bore battery? Your men are manning the guns. We may need you."

"I'll have duties with the hospital but I'll see what I can do. I'll try to catch up."

"Good show. Well, have to find which wagons have our little bit of extra ammunition." He emitted a great sight and shook his head, "I told them to dump tents instead of gunpowder." And giving his horse a nudge, he rode off.

I went in search of Surgeon Major Preston and found him sitting on the seat of one of the wagons. On explaining my desire to march with the men of the 66th who were manning the smoothbore battery, he just grinned.

"Enjoy yourself, Watson. Carter and I will send for you if you're needed."

After gathering some additional medical supplies to my rather overstuffed saddle bags, I gave Murray instructions as to where I would be and for him to stay close to the Surgeon Major so we could find each other. I then went in search of Captain Slade and the smoothbores.

The column was now on the march and I decided to sit on a small swell of ground and have the battery come to me. I watched as Lieutenant Geoghegan and his men left at a trot. His half company of the 3rd Bombay Light Cavalry were evidently to conduct the reconnaissance ahead of the main body. About five minutes elapsed before the next unit came by. It was Captain Mayes squadron of the 3rd Bombay and two guns of Major Blackwood's battery of rifled guns under Lieutenant Maclaine. I had met Maclaine in passing and he appeared a bright fellow but had a reputation as a glory hound.

Now there was a short gap and then came General Nuttall, his staff, more cavalry and two more of Major Blackwood's guns under Lieutenant Fowell. As they passed me, troops of the 3rd Sind Horse took off to left and right of the column to act as flanking guards.

About 100 yards behind was the main column of infantry. The 66th and Jacob's Rifles were on the right, Bombay grenadiers on the left, in the centre, the sappers and miners and the smoothbore battery. The rear guard was made up of the last two cannons of Blackwood's E/B Royal Horse Artillery and some 3rd Sind Horse.

As the main column came abreast of my position, I left my little hillside and trotted over to where Captain Slade rode in advance of this battery of infantry and artillery soldiers. To the right of the main column, moved the baggage trains.

The baggage trains, I knew, were a constant thorn in the side of the line officers. While it had to exist to support our soldiers, it also drained manpower that was needed on the firing line. Each of the three infantry regiments had had to supply a company of soldiers to defend the baggage plus a treasure guard and a commissariat guard. I could see Major Ready of the 66th who commanded this small guard, riding to the left of his columns.

Captain Slade welcomed my salute as I approached the moving guns. "Fit yourself in anywhere, Doctor. You can ride with me for a while if you like."

"Do we know exactly where we're headed?" I inquired.

"Toward the village of Maiwand, Doctor. The Maiwand Pass would give Ayub Khan easy access to Kandahar and we need to plug the bottle, if you will, before Khan can get there. General Burrows believes we should arrive about a day before the old Khan does. We set up a good defence and we'll be able to hold him off... I think."

We rode for a time in silence. The slow pace of the infantry with which we travelled was especially hard on the horses. The natural gait of an artillery horse is a trot. Simple inertia is the problem. Once rolling, it's easier on the horses to keep the 2000 pounds they're pulling moving than have the constant start and stop behind the walking of the infantry. The horses I knew would be tired before the morning had gone.

Matters were made worse by the need for the infantry to stay aligned with the baggage train which moved even more slowly.

As the sun rose higher in the sky, the temperatures rose. By nine in the morning, it was already approaching 100 degrees and we had stopped for the second time to allow the baggage train to close up. While we waited, the artillery drivers watered the horses in a little stream.

I had dismounted and taken Emmett to the stream for a drink when I saw an officer ride up on the far right of the battery and report to Captain Slade. They spoke for a moment, but before I had remounted and returned, he was gone.

"Any news?" I asked, as I returned to Slade's side.

"Oh, no. That was just Lieutenant Dragon. Major Ready has placed him with the few extra rounds of ammunition we have and he wanted to tell me where it was in the column. Good to know. Ah, looks like we're moving again, Doctor. Not covering much ground, are we?"

"Horrible pace. Hurts the horses and the men." I replied.

For the next twenty minutes we walked on until cresting a small knoll. I could see two small villages to our front and another, larger, to our right, some miles off.

"What's the larger village, Captain?"

"That's Maiwand, Doctor. Those two little ones are Mandabad and Khig."

"Seems deserted."

"No, Doctor, they aren't, I assure you. See those dust clouds off to the north? Cavalry. They'll have scouts in the villages. I hope we do."

We continued down the knoll and lost sight of the villages again. By 10 o'clock, we had stopped again when Captain Slade was called forward. I took the time to go among the men and check on their welfare. They were hungry and tired, but the moral was high.

I was talking with Lieutenant Faunce when he suddenly held up his hand and stood in his stirrups, looking to the front. Officers, including Captain Slade, were galloping back to their units. Slade reigned up next to us and called for Lieutenants Jones and Fowle to join us, which they did at the double.

"Well, Gentleman. Looks like we've lost the race. Evidently Ayub Khan is already in Maiwand. We're going to have to attack him immediately if we're to keep him from securing the pass. There is

Afghan cavalry about two and a half miles to the front and infantry probably five miles out."

Just then, the advance was sounded and our column started to move again. The four of us stayed together as the Captain continued. "We'll be moving up the Kushk-i-Nakhud ravine. I can't tell you what's going to happen because I don't know. I do know the old man will pitch into anything he finds. All right then, back to your men. And Doctor, stay close to me. Lieutenant Faunce, send Sergeant Cacy to find Lieutenant Dragon and tell him I want that little bit of ammunition moved to the front of the baggage train."

"Yes, Sir" responded Faunce and saluting, rode back to his division.

As Faunce rode off, I could see the flanking cavalry closing in on the column.

"Why are the flankers closing in?" I asked.

"Keep the column moving faster and keep in closer touch, Doctor. It's a risk, of course. They can't give as early a warning if something happens."

We moved on in silences for a brief while, covered in dust and perspiring in the awful heat. The infantry was suffering greatly with no food and little water, at least their valises were in the baggage. They carried their weapons, water bottles, ammunitions pouches and haversacks. Their khaki uniforms blended with the dust but the black equipment and dark brown puttees made each man of the 66th a target. I suddenly looked down at myself and realized my dark brown Sam Browne belt and boots made the same of me. Captain Slade's voice brought me out of my reverie.

"Something's happening!" he exclaimed, pointing to the left front. "We're moving toward Mandabad toward that dust cloud."

As I looked up, a rider from Major Blackwood's battery was running pall mall at us and barely checked his horse in time to avoid colliding with me. He snapped a salute at Slade.

"Major's compliments, Sir, and would you advance your battery at a trot? The Major will be on the far side of Mandabad across the nala. You're going to come into action on his left, Sir."

"Very good, Corporal. Tell Major Blackwood I understand." With that, the Corporal saluted and was gone.

The air was split by the crack of Blackwood's rifled cannon as we moved at a trot between the engineers and the Bombay infantry. The infantry was now moving at double time and the baggage and hospital were being directed into the nala to provide some protection.

As we crossed the nala, I could see four of Blackwood's guns firing on the Afghan cavalry who were falling back, and in the distance, what seemed to be a forest, truly odd for this area.

As we moved to the left of Blackwood, Slade called "action front" and the battery came into line. Guns were dropped and limbers moved to the rear of the guns. As the men prepared to fire, I could see Lieutenant Osborne's guns coming into action to the right, completing Major Blackwood's battery. Our twelve little guns seemed alone on a vast plain, without cover for man or beast.

The first rounds of cannon fire from the smoothbores were sent at a range of about 1800 yards. It was now, when I saw the trees move, that I realized it wasn't a forest on the distant hills, it was thousands of men! I'm ashamed to say that for a moment, a sense of panic set in. I looked behind and saw our infantry in line, lying on the ground to the rear of the guns. The enemy was well out of rifle shot and lying down afforded our infantry some protection from the enemy cannon. To our right, left and immediate rear, stood the cavalry as flankers for the guns. I could also see Major Ready and Lieutenant Dragon behind the infantry, with our supply of ammunition.

The horde of Afghan infantry was moving to our right as our guns played on them and their cavalry was feeling to our left. A shell burst within a few hundred yards of me. I was no longer a spectator on a great stage. I was a target and the 30 cannons of Ayub's artillery were coming into action.

Emmett, the fine horse he was, stayed steady under my hand and I rode him to the rear of Faunce's division. Here I dismounted, and holding the lead strap, started walking up and down the line looking for who might need assistance.

Captain Slade rode up and down the line, giving each division orders as to how to direct their fire. We were in a fight, cannon against cannon, and we appeared to be outnumbered, probably three to one. While we stood on a barren, flat plain, the Afghans were in what was actually rolling hills, ravines and nalas, which provided cover. It was an uneven match but we were holding our own for the moment. I now had no time to think of the fight, as we were now taking casualties. Handing Emmett's lead strap to a driver, I gathered my saddlebags and ran for Jones' division where the first casualties had occurred.

Lieutenant Jones was between his two guns, giving direction to their aim points. Two of his men were already down and as I ran to them, I could see the drivers cutting a dying horse out of the traces. Fortunately, the plain that made us and the cavalry such a visible target, made us a difficult one also, as the flatness and haze of battle made range prediction difficult.

I was now going man to man, a quick patch and those that could be, were back on the guns. These men of the 66th and Royal Horse were amazing. One would think they were firing on a parade ground. Each round was a smooth load, steady aim, fire.

The artillery battle continued as I moved from gun to gun and wished I'd brought Murray with me. I completely lost track of the overall battle as I worked to bandage and stitch.

It seemed like only moments, but I knew we had been battling for some time when I heard a new sound. It was shell, moving faster and with a heavier explosion than ever before. Slade was nearby and I called to him from the spot where I was bandaging a leg.

"What the Devil is that, Captain?"

Slade walked his horse over and grinned down at me. "Fourteen pounder, breech loading, Armstrong guns, old boy. Bigger and faster than anything we've got. Five rounds a minute, even with an untrained crew. Wish we had them."

"Look, Slade, infantry moving up." I pointed to where our men had risen and were moving forward and establishing themselves to our left and right. To our left came 2 companies of Jacob's Rifles and to our right, the 1st Bombay. I couldn't see the 66th, so I assumed they were somewhere to my right. I went back to my business and now understood the calm of the 66th and Royal Horse. I didn't control the battle, just my part of the battle.

The enemy artillery seemed to increase in intensity. Many horses were going down, the cavalry suffered horribly, unprotected and without the ability to respond to their attackers. At least the artillery could respond with shell.

We had been in the artillery fight for over an hour, when Slade approached me again.

"Doctor, I need you to stay with Lieutenant Faunce. Jones is taking guns to the far right, the 66th is being pressed over there by Ghazis. Fowle is taking his guns to the left of those two companies of the 30th. The 3rd Sind is going to reinforce also, the beggars are trying to flank us with their cavalry. I'm told the baggage guard is being hard pressed too. I'm leaving the seriously wounded here with you and Faunce." With that explanation, he was off, not even waiting for a response. I went back to the wounded. The lack of water was becoming critical. Few could make it across the open plain the mile back to the baggage where water and supplies were plentiful. With them under attack, re-supply was out of the question.

I inspected my watch, 12:45. We'd been at this for two hours now. The Afghans had moved their artillery closer and our casualties continued to mount.

"Does it matter what time it is, Doctor?"

I looked up and there, mounted on a fine bay, was the one-eyed Lieutenant known as Dragon.

"Godard! But I thought.."

"I know what you thought, Doctor! Or more to the point, what you bastards hoped for!" He leaped down from his horse and stood an inch in front of me.

"Left me to die, didn't you! But I didn't, did I?"

I placed my right foot back to gain balance in case of an attack.

"You were ready enough to kill us," I countered.

"I didn't want your life, Doctor, just your treasure. You boys could have shared but you were too good for that! Well, Doctor, you're going to tell me where it is and maybe I won't kill you." He placed his hand on his holster. "In this mess, who's going to notice another body more or less?"

Never before had I seen a man's eye actually glow with hate.

'I should care about what happened to you after you shot Arty? You're lucky I didn't shoot you. You would be dead."

"Arty was an accident. You know that! Leaving me half blinded and at the mercy of the Mohmands, that was no accident!" he spat at me. His body was shaking with rage.

"You're a fool, Godard. And I'll expose your little charade when this is over. Let the pieces fall where they may."

"Doctor Watson, over here, quickly! Sergeant Ryan, if you please, legs gone." It was Lieutenant Faunce.

Godard and I continued to stare at each other.

"Doctor!"

"Coming," I said, taking a step away.

"I'll be back, Doctor!" snorted Godard and turning, mounted his horse and galloped toward the baggage train. I hurried over to Ryan, but it was too late.

The temperature in the afternoon was increasing. Some accounts say the temperature by one o'clock was 120° Fahrenheit, though who had the time to take a reading, I can't imagine. The 1st Bombay on our right and the Jacob's rifles on our left, had been lying on the ground all this time with little to shoot at, but taking horrible casualties from the artillery fire which missed our battery but fell among them.

Fowle and Jones were ordered to re-join with Faunce as their ammunition ran low. It was as they re-joined us, I was called to Lieutenant Fowle who had been wounded severely in the leg. I was able to stop the bleeding and one of the soldiers helped me to get him back on his horse. He wanted to stay but Captain Slade ordered him off the field. I gave his horse's lead strap to a driver who no longer had a team and saw him off. I was now down to almost no medical supplies. By now, half the horses were dead and a good fourth of the men, dead or wounded.

One by one, our six guns fell silent. Slade had been right at the Helmand. The officers had tents, but we had no ammunition!

Captain Slade called Osborne and Faunce to the centre of the battery.

"We've no ammunition wagons to supply us, Osborne. Take the battery to the rear, find Lieutenant Dragon, he has a few rounds in the supply wagons, get them and return as quickly as you can. I'm going to Major Blackwood to see where he wants us next." The three saluted and dispersed.

Having empty saddlebags, I mounted Emmett, who, up to now had been untouched by the chaos around us. As the battery limbered up the guns, I could see the faces of the men of Jacob's Rifles to our left. It was a look of dismay. You didn't have to hear the voices, the question was plain. "Where are the guns going?" "Why are they leaving us?" The enemy was now in rifle range and the guns were pulling out. You could smell the fear.

The ground rumbled as we rode for the baggage train. The dust was so thick I could hardly see. The wounded occupied every spare inch of the limbers and guns.

Suddenly, I found myself on the ground, laying face down. I was dazed. As I tried to pick myself up from the ground, I felt a weakness in my left shoulder. I couldn't get it to respond. Rolling to my right, I tucked my legs up and got off the ground. There was blood pouring down my left arm and all I could seem to do was look at it.

"Bloody shame you were wounded, old boy. Could have been killed, you know. How does it feel?

It'll hurt much more when they try to fix it. The doctors are such butchers here. Maybe they'll just take it off."

It was Godard, on his bay, with his pistol in his right hand, pointing at me and grinning like a madman.

"Damn you, Godard! We're fighting for our lives here!"

"Doesn't bother me, Doctor. I'm already dead." He grinned again and a strange laugh emanated from his throat. "Now, tell me, where did you put the treasure?"

"Damned if I'll tell you after you shot me!"

"Makes no difference to me, John. If you don't tell me and die, 'en combat', shall we say, there's always your boy Murray. Probably give it up quite easily when he learns of your demise, facing the enemy and all, what?"

Shells were landing closer and closer as the Afghans pressed around us but neither of us paid any attention.

"I'm asking one last time, Doctor." He cocked the hammer of his revolver.

Again, I found myself on the ground. The concussion from a shell had thrown me to the ground. It had landed behind Godard and he and his horse were down. The animal, screaming in pain, was trying to rise but could not. His right foreleg was gone and his hind legs were tangled in his entrails. Shell fragments had ripped open his belly and spilled his insides out.

Godard was trying to pull his right leg from under the horse, trying to get away from the flailing hooves. Without thinking, I picked myself up and ran forward. Putting my one good arm under his shoulder, pulled him free. We fell back in a heap and I scrambled back to my feet. Godard bounded up, pistol still in his hand.

"Thanks, John. But that changes nothing." Taking his pistol, he turned to his horse and putting his pistol to the animal's head ended its pain. Turning back to me, he re-cocked it and pointed it at my head.

"Now, John, for the last time. Where is the treasure?"

But in the time it took him to turn from his horse I was on him. It seemed to be a bizarre struggle. A one armed man against a man with one eye. I grabbed the barrel of his revolver and twisted it away from me but he still held tight to the grip. I pushed into him and the two of us went down falling over his horse. We were covered in blood and entrails yet we still rolled about the dirt each struggling for survival. Godard was using his free hand to try and get at my eyes, tucking my head down I smashed into his nose and he released the pistol, but I couldn't hold onto it. The slime of the dead horse had made everything slick. Godard pushed me away and scrambled to his feet searching for the weapon. It was only a yard or two away, dropping on one knee he picked up the pistol and turned to me with that insane grin.

I fired three times in rapid succession. Godard went down in a heap. So intent had he been on finding his weapon he never saw me draw my revolver when he was turned away.

I stood up and went over to where Godard lay. There was no doubt, this time he was dead. "It didn't have to end this was, Godard. It was only jewels. Now you've lost the only real treasure."

I looked for Emmett but could not find him, so I trotted as best I could for the baggage train. It seemed like forever but I finally reached the comparative safety of the nala. The three companies with the baggage trains had been engaged for some time as the enemy pressed down the nala from direction of Maiwand.

As I stumbled into the hospital, I called out for Murray. It was only a moment until he found me and was taking me to Surgeon Major Preston. As he helped me forward, I was surrounded by other wounded. Murray sat me on a stool and removed my tunic. Preston obviously tired and worn from treating the wounded looked at my shoulder.

"Not too bad, Watson. No exit wound and there is not time to get it out now. We'll stop the bleeding and get you some rest."

As he dressed the wound, I could still hear the crack of Blackwood's guns and the musket fire had become general. Men from the 66th baggage guard were holding the Ghazis back in the nala and the other two companies tried to keep the cavalry off our left and ghazis off our right.

As Preston bandages my wound, my mind was racing. What would I do about Godard? Surely it would never come back to me, and I had only defended myself, but the whole tragedy of the treasure seemed to be suffocating me.

"Watson. Watson! Answer me!"

It was Preston. "Are you alright? I thought we were losing you for a minute. You seemed to stop breathing."

"I'm fine, really." I sputtered out. "Just thirsty and tired."

Murray gave me a water bottle and I drank copiously.

"Now, give me my blouse and belt."

Murray hesitated and looked at Preston. Preston nodded and Murray helped me.

"Stay with me, Murray, and you can help be my hands. Lots of wounded here." My shoulder ached but movement was better than sitting and we started making the rounds. I saw the smoothbore battery to our left and went to check on our men. They had fired the only two rounds they had at the Afghan rifles to try to protect their guns. We passed through the ranks doing what we could and returned to the hospital to find Surgeon Major Preston being bandaged by Surgeon Carter. Preston had taken a bullet in the hip and was unable to walk. Murray helped place him on a doolie when I realized something – The artillery. It was still firing but the rate had slackened. Were the Afghans running out of ammunition? Climbing the bank of the nala, I looked toward the plain and the fighting beyond. To my horror, I could see Blackwood's battery moving toward us, then stopping at the ammunition wagons to re-supply. None of our guns were firing. Herati Infantry and Ghazis were pouring through our lines! The Jacob's Rifles that had been on our left and the Bombay Infantry on our right were no longer there. What appeared to be a wave of running infantry was rolling to the right toward the 66th with little ripples of waves heading straight toward us. Our lines had completely broken! I could see our cavalry to the left form in a loose knot and charge toward the centre, then swing right and toward us. In a moment, they were forming to the left of the nala as Blackwood's battery came in sans two guns. Blackwood wasn't with them and Slade was commanding. Slade unlimbered and started firing into the Afghan cavalry and infantry and ghazis. Men of all units ran into the hospital and baggage train and formed up where they could. Colonel Griffith gathered a small force of the 1st Bombay and they formed up with the company of the 66th and men of Jacob's rifles in a mud-walled enclosure. General Burrows now came in riding double with the Wordi Major of the 3rd Sind Horse, having given his horse to a wounded officer. Burrows ordered us to fall back and Captain Slade formed the rear guard with his cannon. The doolie bearers and the like deserted in a whole sale manner.

Murray and I frantically helped the wounded onto every conveyance we could find. Every limber and gun of the 66th's smoothbore battery carried the wounded out. Preston's doolie bearers left him on the ground, but we were able to get him on a gun limber. A thousand men were gone and we were fleeing for our lives.

The artillerymen and a portion of Major Ready's baggage guard were the only units who appeared to maintain their formation and discipline. The retreat to Kandahar was on in earnest

Chapter 20

There was no stemming the flood of the rout. Mixed groups of followers and sepoys, dismounted sowars and soldiers streamed away from Mandabad. Lieutenant E. Monteith had formed a handful of his sowars on the left bank while Slade, whose artillery had kept their formation and nerve, continued to fire. The two groups covered our work to get the wounded loaded on pony or horse, camel or bullock, anything we could find. In the meantime, General Burrows had ordered the few men of the 66th, along with a few of Jacob's Rifles and 1st Bombay to retire from their enclosure so as not to be left behind.

At the time, neither Burrows nor any of the rest of us knew of the desperate fight of the 66th going on a mile distant at Khig, where they had fallen back. It would be days before anyone knew what happened.

It was now, as we tried to load the wounded, that I was felled by the second bullet. For the third time that day, I found myself on the ground. My left leg, just above the knee, had taken a bullet. As it turned out, it was from a Snider. Whether a misdirected round from our own men, from a deserter of the Wali's Army or a weapon taken from a dead sepoy, I'm sure I will never know.

It was Murray who was standing by me when it happened. He was holding the lead of a cart pony. Reaching down, he grabbed me by the belt as I had once grabbed him, he helped me rise on my one good leg. I grabbed at the pony's harness to steady myself.

The last gun of Slade's battery was limbering to move. The infantry was gone and Monteith's few troopers were surrounding Slade's gun. If we didn't move with them, we would be at the mercy of the Ghazis. With a super-human effort, Murray half lifted, half pushed me upon the pony's back. Pain screamed through my leg and up my spine, light blinded my eyes and I almost passed out. It was the terror of falling into the hands of the Ghazis that kept me going and able to hold the harness saddle to stay on the pony.

"Hold on Sir! Hold on! We're staying with the guns no matter what! Don't worry, Sir! Don't you worry, Sir! I got you!"

I looked in Murray's worried eyes but all I could do was nod as we moved off.

We weaved through the mass of moving men and animals, toward our last camp at Kushk-i-Nakhud. As Murray led us along, we sought out the guns, whatever safety there might be, would be with them. In a short time we were able to find Lieutenant Faunce and the men of the 66th with the smoothbores. Every inch of his limbers and guns were covered with wounded. Having no ammunition, he was doing all he could to use his ordnance and horses to transport those who could not walk. Just behind us came the guns of Blackwood's battery commanded by Captain Slade. What had become of Blackwood, I didn't know. Slade, seeing me, rode over and stopped momentarily.

"Doctor, how bad is it?"

"I'll be all right, bleeding is stopped. When halt somewhere Carter will patch it up. Where's Blackwood?"

"He was wounded and couldn't ride. Last I saw, he was with Colonel Galbraith on the right with the 66th." He looked at the ground, then back at me and smiled. "Perhaps he'll be in yet. Too much of a mess to know who's where." Pulling back on the reigns and watching as we walked on, he called out. "Stay with the guns, old man. Stay with the guns." Turning his horse to the rear, he trotted back to the battery. We pressed on towards the old camp ground.

Here, I will comment on the contradictions which I saw in General Burrows. I will never understand the man. A man who had given his own horse to a wounded fellow officer but who now abandoned us. Colonel St. John had been to our old camp and back. There was plenty of water and the men had been without water or food for 24 hours. True, some had already passed the old camp but a few minutes stop to water horses and men was much needed. The next water was 15 miles distant at Hauz-i-Madat on the Kandahar road. Burrows however ordered our column on, past the camp and to keep moving. He, in the meanwhile, took the remnants of Nuttall's cavalry on a 7 mile ride to Ata Karez where they watered and rested, leaving Captain Slade and Major Leach to drive on exhausted men and animals, and taking away manpower and carbines needed to defend the rear of the column. Major Leach was right on his later criticisms of the retreat.

More infantry now gathered around the guns as we continued on to Hauz-i-Madat. Night came on and had it not been for Major Leach's knowledge of the area, we may well have never found the tanks there and died on the Afghan plain. As it turned out, General Burrows and the cavalry had been ahead of us, but had not sent anyone out to guide us to the wells in the late darkness. It was nigh on 11 p.m. before we found the water.

For the next two hours, men and animals shared the small tanks of water. It was here that Surgeon Carter was able to clean and dress my wounds. I will be forever grateful.

All that two hours, men and animals came in. The tanks were a good quarter mile from Hauz-i-Madat and General Burrows now ordered the cavalry to continue the march toward Kandahar. It was Major Leach who took 5 sowars and rode back to the tanks to gather the men there so they wouldn't be left behind.

We were not being pressed by any organized enemy at this point. The occasional local with a Jizail or matchlock was all that occurred. It would be days before we would find out that Ayub Khan had won a tactical, but not strategic, victory. While we had been driven from the field with the loss of almost 1,000 men, he had suffered almost 5,000 casualties, killed and wounded. His Ghazis would leave by the thousands to take their wounded and dead home to their villages. It would be days before he could move on Kandahar. But the fear of an organized pursuit was all too real to us. As the hours wore on, we realized we had only to fear each village as we passed.

The cannons at Hauz-i-Madat were joined by Lieutenant Goeghegan and his men of the 3rd Bombay Light Horse. They were to stay with the guns as we waited for the last of the men to come back from water. The gun horses were giving out and before we left Hauz-i-Madat, one gun was spiked and left along with a spare carriage and the store limber wagon.

As we moved out of Hauz-i-Madat, the cavalry, less Geoghegan's men, moved to the front travelling at a pace neither the men nor the worn out artillery horses could keep. The gap between us kept getting wider and grew to three miles or more. It was five in the morning when we reached Ashikan. The cavalry had long been there and were well watered and rested. I was barely able to ride and had taken more than one does of laudanum. Murray was footsore and tired and I begged him to ride a limber for awhile. He refused.

At Ashikan, two more guns were spiked and abandoned and General Burrows ordered the cavalry to give up horses to the artillery so that the limbers of wounded could move on. Burrows was full of conflicting messages!

We marched on through the early morning light and still we received the occasional shot here and there. At Sinjiri, we reached the river Arghandab. While the river was low, it was still a dangerous crossing for men and animals that had fought a battle and been on the move for over a day. Again, a gun had to be spiked and abandoned when it became bogged down in the river bed. It was here too, that we were met by Lieutenant Anderson and sowars of the Poona Horse. They had been sent from Kandahar for our relief and to escort us through the hostile villages. A few miles on, we met the infantry and artillery of the relief column. They gathered the wounded and helped us on. Poor Slade would have to abandon one more smoothbore to save horses and the cargo of wounded carried by the limbers before we reached the citadel of Kandahar.

It was 2:30 in the afternoon when we reached the cantonment, about a half hour behind the cavalry. We had been on the move for over 33 hours and had gone 45 miles with wounded men who had little water and no food for more than two days. It was a miracle!

My time at Kandahar is somewhat of a blank. I was taken within the citadel to the hospital, along with Surgeon Major Preston and about 173 other soldiers and followers. The hospital was well supplied and in good order. I have only the best to say of the surgeons, warders, writers and others of the medical department. Murray stayed with me every moment. Another surgeon, I'm afraid I don't know his name, was able to remove both bullets on the evening of the 28th. I thought I was out of danger. I was wrong. During the next few days, I lay in a bed next to Preston. He was excellent company, with never a discouraging comment or unpleasant word to anyone. I was vaguely aware of the bustle around us as we lay there. The garrison was preparing for the inevitable arrival of Ayub Khan and his army.

Chapter 21

On the day following our arrival at Kandahar, I awoke to find Murray sitting on a stool next to my bed.

"Feeling better, Sir?" he asked with a grin.

"Yes." I replied. "Just weak. But what are you doing here? You're the one who should be resting; after all, I rode all the way."

Murray chuckled. "I'll get you something to eat, Sir. You need it."

"Wait a moment. Murray, give me your hand." I reached up from the bed. He looked at me a bit quizzically, but extended his own.

"Murray, I owe you my life. I'll never forget that. Someday, I hope to repay the debt."

Murray looked like he felt, a bit overwhelmed, as he shook my hand. "You did the same for me, Sir. Guess that makes us even." We clasped hands for a moment more then he stepped back. "Well, Sir, about those victuals. I'll see to it right off, Sir." And he turned and left.

"Afraid you have a friend for life there," came a voice from the next bed. I turned and looked at the smiling face of Surgeon Major Preston.

"Yes," I replied. "Murray is a good man. We need a few million more like him in this Army."

"We'll certainly need them. The powers that be have sent every Durani out of the citadel for fear of having to fight enemies inside and outside at the same time. Afraid it's just us and the Indian Army now."

"Surely there will be a relief column from India."

"Oh, I'm sure, Watson. But will they arrive in a timely manner? That will be the question."

"I have faith."

"So do I, Doctor," he said, leaning back in the bed and looking to the ceiling. "And I'll pray every day," and he turned and winked at me.

I'm afraid that day was my last clear recollection for the next four weeks. It is a terrible thing in a way to be a doctor. You know what's wrong with you when it happens and yet you can't prevent it. By the second day, I knew I was in the first stages of enteric fever. How did I contract it? The better question was how could I not? Horses, camels, bullocks and men had been forced to drink from a single source of water. And while I knew that the death rate was only about sixty-five in 100,000, that was in a fairly healthy population. I was not a healthy population. Weakened as I was from my two wounds and lack of food and water, mine was a risky case. The possibility of infection of the wounds combined with the enteric fever gave me pause to think hard of my own mortality.

As the garrison built additional defences, Surgeon Major Preston and Murray tried to cheer me. I'm afraid that I remember no more for the next four weeks. In my fever and delusions, I fought with Ghazis and Heratis, cannons manned by the 66th blazed and I killed Godard time and time again. In my few lucid moments, I felt sure of my own demise. While the men of the 66th and the Kandahar garrison fought for all our lives, I fought for my own. The month of August, 1880, is literally unknown to me.

It was the 29th of August when, having survived the fever, I next have a clear recollection. Doctor Preston was no longer my roommate, having returned to partial duty, but Murray was there, sitting on the same stool beside my bed, when my mind finally cleared.

"Murray," I croaked, holding out a hand. "Have I been sick long?"

"Why no, Sir. It wasn't even a month until tomorrow."

"A month?" I couldn't even recognize my own voice. It sounded dry and parched. "Water, please."

"Here, Sir" and he held my head off the pillow. "Missed quite a bit, you have, Sir. Been a regular donnybrook, it has."

He gave me a drink and put my head back down. "Almost over now, Sir. Relief column is at Robat. Been getting regular heliograph messages now. Must be ten thousand men coming to help is what I hear."

"We've held out then."

"Yes, Sir. Fight here and there, of course. Nothing to worry about. You get some more rest now."

The next morning, the 30th of August, I was feeling very weak but knew I was going to be all right. My wounds had mended well considering my debilitated state. I continued to have periods of shaking and both my leg and arm would spasm, but I knew I would live. Murray supplied me with the most welcome of all news; General Roberts was only twelve miles from Kandahar and would arrive the next day. Much cheered by this news, I insisted on trying to get up, and with a good crutch and Murray, I made a slow round of the hospital. I was greeted well by the other doctors and everyone appeared in good cheer with relief so close. In less than an hour, I was back abed, thoroughly worn out.

It was early the next morning when I was awakened by the news of General Robert's arrival and I insisted that Murray help me to the citadel walls. As we took the steps to the parapet by the Shikarpur gate, I could hear the skirl of the pipes of the 92nd Highlanders. Never a more beautiful sound had I ever heard. I sat for the better part of the morning on the parapet wall watching the arrival of even more troops and lost in my own thoughts. It was only Murray's kind voice that finally broke the spell as the heat intensified and we returned to hospital about noon.

Evening was coming when Surgeon Major Preston limped into my room. The hospital had been busy all day, for while the relief column was overall in good spirit and health, they had marched some 230 miles in 20 days and had a sizable sick list.

"Watson, good to see you've been up and about. Brought you something," and from a pocket, he pulled a flask and two small cups. Sitting on Murray's stool, he poured out two measures and handed one to me.

"Thought you might want to know what's going on. At least know what I know, that is." He took a drink, as did I, and he started to tell me of the size of Robert's force and the plans for battle on the morrow. Our four remaining companies of the 66th would be used as a holding force out on Picquet Hill while Robert's men, along with a strong force from Kandahar, enveloped Ayub Khan's force and tried to cut off any retreat.

"Oh, I don't pretend to understand tactics, my boy," smiled the old man. "I just patch them up so they can go back to doing what they're doing."

"What are we doing?" I asked. "I mean, here, in Afghanistan. What have we accomplished?"

"Now don't go getting queer on me, Watson." He patted my shoulder and poured us each another whiskey. "If we keep Afghanistan from the Russians, we keep India intact. Simple as that."

"I suppose," I replied and thanked him for all his kindness during my illness. Murray had told me how Preston had checked on me day and night.

"Watson, you're not making this easy for me." He looked down at the tin cup in his hands. "There has been a board of the medical officers here and it's been decided that you need to return to England. I'm afraid active campaigning is out of the question for you now. It's really for the best, my boy. After General Roberts rids us of Ayub Khan, you'll be going home. I envy you in a way. Been a long time since I've seen home."

I was stunned. I never imagined this would happen. But in my heart, I knew he was right. My leg, especially, would never be the same. I was filled with an unimaginable sadness. I said not another word and finally Preston sighed and promising to return in the morning, he left me to my thoughts.

That next morning, Murray appeared early as usual and I convinced him to take me back up on the parapet wall. From here, we could watch as our forces deployed against Ayub Khan and his minions. The destruction of Ayub Khan's army took less than four hours. The artillery opened the assault at 9:30 and by 1 o'clock, Major General Ross was in possession of the Sardar's camp and ordnance, to include the two guns of Blackwood's battery that had been lost at Maiwand. As I returned to my bed there was general rejoicing in all of Kandahar. Ayub Khan's army of 15,000 was scattered to the wind and he was on the run. As Murray helped me back to the hospital I decided to ask his help one more time.

"Murray, I've got to get to Dakka. Will you help me?"

Without a moment's hesitation he responded, "Yes, Sir, of course. Soon as you're able to travel, Sir."

"I'm able to go now."

Murray looked askance at me. "Yes, Sir. If you say so. We'll have to find a convoy, Get some passage south."

"You leave that to me, Murray." And smiling to myself, I went to bed and took a nap.

Later that night Preston appeared again. His smiling face trying to hide his concern for my welfare. "Great things today, Watson. Great things. We'll be able to get you home soon. Afghanistan will be a safe place, you know."

"Yes, Doctor," I smiled, putting on my best face. "I'd like to be on the first transport out. Murray can help me to Karachi and then return to the 5th. I suppose they're still in Jalalabad."

Preston was a little taken aback by my enthusiasm but agreed to find out what he could about any movement going south. I had not long to wait.

The morning brought mixed news. General Robert's victory had indeed been decisive, over 600 dead ghazis were buried between Kandahar and Pir Paimal and no remnants of an army could be found. This was great news. But in the abandoned camp of Ayub Khan was found the body of Lieutenant Maclaine of Blackwood's battery. He had been captured during our retreat and foully murdered in the last moments of the battle the day prior.

It was Preston who brought me the news I really wanted. Major Evan Smith, a political officer, was taking elements of the 3rd Bombay Cavalry and 19th Bombay Infantry to open communications with General Phayre whose column was coming up from the south. I would leave tomorrow.

By the 5th of September, Murray and I were well on our way to Quetta and then Sibi and the train. It would take 14 days on native ponies moving with small detachments from place to place to complete the journey. We were more than half way one night and I was feeling none too well when Murray queried me about my intentions when we got to Dakka.

"Sir. If you don't mind, I'd like to know what we do when we get the treasure."

"I guess it's pretty obvious why we're going there," I replied. "I've not made up my mind entirely though. I just know I can't leave it there. Too many lives have been spent on it. It has to do some good."

Murray looked somewhat relieved. "Yes, Sir. Hoping you were going to say that." He was quiet for a moment, staring into the fire at our little camp. "Sir," he finally said. "I know about Lieutenant Godard." The hair went up on my neck and my muscles stiffened. I said nothing. "It was while you had the fever, Sir. You talked about it over and over."

I looked into the fire, not daring to speak for a moment. "Does anyone else know?"

"Yes, Sir. Surgeon Major Preston. He told me to be quiet about it, but I wouldn't have said nothing anyway. He said he knew a way to get you out of here and back to England. I never told him about the treasure. He knew that Lieutenant Godard tried to kill you and you was just defending yourself, but he thought it be best for you to get away from here."

I tried to stretch my tensed up muscles. So, that was the reason for the short work on the medical board. Preston was looking out for me!

"Murray, I've decided what to do with the treasure."

"Well, that's fine, Sir. If you don't need anything, I'll be calling it a night."

"Good Night, Murray." I lay back with my pipe and thought way into the night.

From Sibi, we were able to entrain as if going to Karachi but we left the train at the junction in Ruk and got on another headed to Jhelum. I had thought that might be a problem since our orders didn't take us that way, but it was simplicity itself. Non one even questioned a wounded surgeon and his orderly but accepted what I said. Once in Jhelum, it was again simple to get with a column leaving for Peshawar. We had been on the road for 28 days when we finally arrived in Peshawar back with the Khyber Field Force.

The 25th of October was a horribly busy day. I had acquired ponies at Jhelum but I now needed a reason to get to Dakka. I still had kit in Jalalabad, not much of a reason, but it would have to do..

"Well, Sir," advised Murray, as we sat pondering our strategy. "Don't the native clinic need extra supplies maybe and we're going to bring them afore you leave?"

So with Murray's brilliant suggestion and my grovelling in the hospital at Peshawar, the next morning we left with a patrol of the 13th Bengal Cavalry and three pack mules full of medical supplies.

The countryside was now extremely peaceful. Since the defeat of Ayub Khan and his retreat to Herat, it seems the fight had gone out of the Afghans. That, with the infusion of money from the Indian government brought quiet, if not peace, to the area.

We spent the first night at Jamrud where four companies of the 5th were and had a fine reunion with Surgeon Major Bennett, Colonel Rowland and the rest. They kept me up long into the night wanting all the details of Maiwand and Kandahar and the great battles. It was here that I first came up with the falsehood of the Jizail Ballet. It was perfectly believable and readily accepted, and so, it became "the truth".

We pressed on, all the way to Dakka the next day, riding in at early evening. Here too was a company of the 5th and numerous companies of the 27th Punjab. But our first stop was the clinic outside the gates. We hoped there would still be someone there and I found myself moving more and more quickly in hopes of finding Malalai.

And there she was. An assistant surgeon of the 27th by the name of Banks had taken over the operation. As Murray and I dismounted, I could see him and Malalai, inside conversing and two ward men were loading a mule with supplies to be taken back to the fort for the night.

I handed my pony's reigns to Murray. "Wait here a moment, Murray. We probably just need to hand these mules off. No need to unpack."

I walked into the little clinic. "Malalai." I said sternly, "Come here, I need you." Both Banks and Malalai turned to look at me and before I could breathe, she was in my arms and crushing me with an embrace. Poor Banks looked stunned as it took me a moment to dislodge myself from the crushing embrace and saw the flow of tears on her face.

"Here, here." I said soothingly. "Sit down on the bench. I'm afraid I gave you a fright." She sat on the bench but would not release my hand and continued to sob. I looked at Banks. "The name is John Watson," I smiled, "and I usually don't have this effect on women!"

"Ah, now I understand. She talks about you all the time. Seems you're her hero." He smiled down at the girl as she tried to compose herself. "But, you see, we thought you were dead, killed at Maiwand, you know."

"Well," I said, touching Malalai's shoulder with my good hand, "I don't believe I was. Wounded, yes. Killed, no!" As Malalai gained control of herself, I gave an uncomfortable laugh.

"How have you been Malalai?"

"I've been wonderful, Doctor. More now. I told you killed. Many killed."

"Yes, but thanks to Murray not me. We've brought you supplies for the clinic," I said, addressing myself to Banks. "They're outside with my orderly."

"Ah, well, I'll have my men take them back in the fort. We can always use more, back in a moment." So saying, he stepped outside.

Malalai had controlled her tears for now and smiled up at me, still holding my hand. She was indeed lovely, and intelligent, and kind and all the rest.

She looked at the ground as she said, "You must come and see my husband tonight."

Suddenly, there was a heavy weight in my chest. "Your husband?"

"Yes, Guhkta. He and I marry last week. He is a good man."

I regret that I let out an audible sigh, but catching myself, I picked her up by the shoulders and looking down into her dark eyes, I told her how luck she and Guhkta were and how proud I was to have been able to play a part in their lives.

"Ready, Sir. Hello, Miss." It was Murray at the door. "Handed off the mules, Sir. We'd best get on to the fort. Doctor Banks wants you to meet him at the officer's mess."

"Yes, coming Murray. Malalai, I will see you again before I leave. Congratulations on your marriage. I wish you only the best."

That night was spent much as the previous one and it was all I could do to answer the plethora of questions about Maiwand. Many of the questions, I simply did not know the answers to: Why the line broke? Why the cavalry was so ineffective? Why the lack of reconnaissance? I could only answer as to what I saw. Toward the end of the evening, I approached Banks and asked for the loan of his hospital warder, Guhkta for a day. To this request, he was only too happy to oblige.

So, armed with the carbines and mounted on 3 good ponies, Murray, Guhkta and I left Dakka Fort in the pre-dawn light headed for the second cross. Murray and I never told Guhkta where we were going or why. The listener to this story will be greatly disappointed that the trip was completely uneventful. Within six hours, we had travelled to the cross and returned. In the saddlebag of my pony rested the small coffer of jewels and the icon that had stood on the shelf with it. Having sent Guhkta to the stables with Murray, I went to the small room I'd been given as temporary quarters and spread the contents of the saddlebag on the bunk. I looked again, amazed, at the enormous wealth of rubies and diamonds.

I separated about 10 per-cent of the jewels as best I could estimate and put them in a chamois bag for Murray. Then I did the same for Guhkta and Malalai and once more deposited the 10 per-cent in a chamois bag. The rest I put back in the coffer. I knew what Arty wanted done with his share and I knew what I would do with mine and Sturt's. The only thing left was to get to Bombay and home, well, at least to England. I was wearing down and I knew it. The gruelling pace of the last month and the debilitated condition of my health had taken its toll. I just wanted to be somewhere and rest.

Outside the walls that afternoon, I bought a small decorative box. Its designs meant nothing to me but the local said it was for weddings so I paid my rupees and took it back to the fort where I placed the chamois bag for Guhkta and Malalai inside. I sent Murray to find Guhkta. He returned quickly with Guhkta at his side. I presented Guhkta with the box and had him promise not to open it for six months.

"If the Surgeon sahib does not wish it, I will not."

"Guhkta, you are the luckiest of men and this will only add to your good fortune." I smirked as I said the words. "You will do me the greatest of considerations by doing as I ask."

"Of course, Sir." We shook hands.

"Tell your wife that you and she will forever be my friends and I wish you many children and a long life."

"Of course, sahib, and for you, our house is always open."

Taking the box, Guhkta left.

Murray and I departed the following morning with the 13th on its return patrol to Peshawar, arriving on the 11th and were able to form up with a column leaving for Jhelum on the 13th. But during our two days at Peshawar, my curiosity got the better of me. Where was Colonel Enderby? I had fully expected he would hear of my return and would somehow interfere with my plans by attempting to way lay me. To my delight, my enquiry as to his whereabouts resulted in the knowledge that he had been transferred to the Kurram Valley. To this day, I do not know if he was behind Godard going to Kandahar but I find it hard to believe he was not.

By the night of the 26th of October, 1880, Murray and I were in Karachi and boarded ship for Bombay. He would only be with me a few more days and so on our last night before reaching Bombay, I asked him to come to my cabin as I wanted to speak to him privately.

"What can I do for you, Sir?"

"Ah, it's what I can do for you, Murray." I went to my kit and extracted the chamois bag with his share of the treasure and handed it to him.

"This is little enough, Murray. Especially as I owe you my life."

"Why you don't owe me nothing, Sir. You took care of me, I took care of you. That's all."

"Well here."

"No, Sir, I can't. I suspect I know what you're going to do with that and my share goes too."

"No, Murray, you can't."

"Why, Sir? What do I need that for? Don't I get fed and a place to sleep and clothes? Oh, and a little excitement now and then? Don't need the bother, Sir. Put it with the rest."

I had mixed emotion of frustration and pride in my fellow man.

"Well, here." I reached in the bag and pulling out a large ruby, placed it in his hand. "I'll do what you ask. But on the condition that you take this. Let's say for in case of emergency."

Murray looked at the stone in his hand, gave a little nod and said, "All right, Sir. In case of emergency. But you must do the likewise."

I laughed and reaching in the bag, took out another ruby and placing it in my pocket, said "In case of emergency."

So we shook hands and said good night.

On arriving in Bombay, I found my luck was holding as the Orontes was to sail for England in two days and I, having been wounded at Maiwand and medically released, had priority on sailing. There was only one more task to accomplish. So I set off in search of my final goal.

The Catholic community in Bombay was exceedingly small, compared to the native religions. For almost 100 years the British Government had continuously inserted itself as an obstacle to the growth of the church for fear of Papal influence on the natives. It was a poor community of Capuchin Fathers who oversaw the Bombay Vicariate which extended from Bombay to Kabul and the Punjab. It was quite an impossible task.

So it was to the complete consternation of one Father O'Callahan that a British Army Surgeon handed over a coffer of jewels worth a King's Ransom, a 17th century icon and an assurance that both were church property.

The flabbergasted Padre wanted to know everything, but I was tired and for the first time in a long time, felt relieved of a tremendous burden. So despite his protestations and with the briefest of explanations and the further gift of Sturt's map, I left Father O'Callahan and spent my last night in India at Watson's Hotel. The next morning I boarded the Orontes. The passage home was indeed tedious and more than once I wondered what I was to do next? England? Australia? The United States and my only family? Where should I end up?

Murray and I had said farewell on the docks and I have only seen him two or three times over the years. I shall be sad never to see him again.

Chapter 22

"The rest, Holmes, you know."

"Amazing, Watson! You've had more than a lifetime of adventure!" Holmes rose from his chair by the fire and placed his pipe on the mantel. Crossing to the window he drew back the drapes, the sun shown brightly into the room.

"Oh, Holmes. I've kept you up all night with my silly talking!"

"On the contrary, my friend. It has been an amazing tale of a very courageous man. You're a kind man and a great friend"

"If you say so." I blustered. "Perhaps we'd best try for some sleep."

"No, I for one am not tired at all; perhaps you'll ring Mrs Hudson for some breakfast."

"Yes, I think that would do." As I pulled the bell rope, I saw Holmes looking out the window.

"And the medal? How did Murray come in possession of it? I presume it was given to you for the kind 'donation', shall we say?"

"Oh, It was given to me here, back when we had first taken rooms together. We had not yet become friends. In fact, at the time, I wasn't sure we would. You seemed the oddest of characters and I had no idea of your business. Most of all, it brought back sad memories so I sent it on to Murray with a note saying he deserved it as much as I."

"Since the ruby was in Murray's box to you, I assume no emergency ever arose for its use. And yours?"

I turned to the desk and removed from the top left drawer a small Bakelite box with a Celtic Cross engraved on the lid. I handed it to Holmes. Opening it, he found another ruby similar to the first. "Ah, again, no emergency." He returned the box to me and putting it with Murray's, I placed them in the drawer as a tapping came on our door. It opened and Mrs Hudson asked if we were ready for breakfast. I was about to answer when Holmes interrupted.

"Not yet, Mrs Hudson, but be good enough to bring up some tea for four if you would."

"Certainly, Sir," replied Mrs Hudson and departed.

"Holmes?"

"Growler outside, Watson. Man and a woman talking. He's not sure about coming up but she'll convince him. Banker I should say. She's a governess. Yes, she's convinced him. Be good enough to get the door for Mrs Hudson, would you, Watson?"

"Holmes."

"Yes, Watson?"

"I'm glad my Afghan adventure led me here."

Holmes grinned. "As am I Watson, as am I!"

Also from MX Publishing:

Molly Carr

In Search of Dr.Watson – A Sherlockian Investigation

The definitive biography of Dr.Watson

www.mxpublishing.co.uk

Also from MX Publishing:

 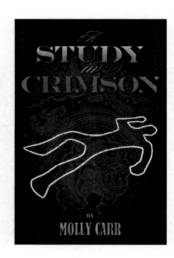

Molly Carr

The Sign of Fear
And
A Study In Crimson

The first two adventures of Mrs.Watson with a supporting cast including Sherlock Holmes, Dr.Watson and Moriarty

www.mxpublishing.co.uk

Also from MX Publishing:

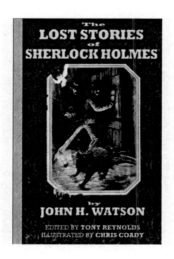

John H Watson

Edited by Tony Reynolds

The recent decease of one of the descendents of Dr. Watson has brought to light his personal papers. These include a number of stories that Dr. Watson suppressed at the time for various reasons. As all involved are long dead, the inheritor has agreed to the publication of a set of eight of the most interesting adventures.

www.mxpublishing.co.uk

Also from MX Publishing:

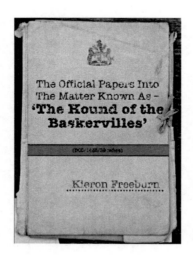

Kieron Freeburn

The Official Papers Into The Matter Known As The Hound of the Baskervilles (DCC/1435/89 refers)

The original police papers from the Hound of The Baskervilles case discovered by real-life 'Sherlock Holmes', former Metropolitan Police detective Kieron Freeburn.

www.mxpublishing.co.uk

Also from MX Publishing:

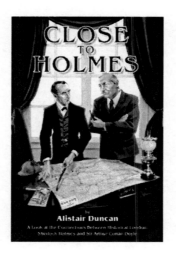

Alistair Duncan

Close To Holmes

A Look at the Connections Between Historical London, Sherlock Holmes and Sir Arthur Conan Doyle

www.mxpublishing.co.uk

Also from MX Publishing:

Alistair Duncan

Eliminate the Impossible

An Examination of the World of Sherlock Holmes on Page and Screen

www.mxpublishing.co.uk

Also from MX Publishing:

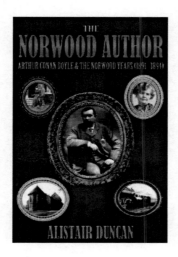

Alistair Duncan

The Norwood Author

**Arthur Conan Doyle
and the Norwood Years (1891 - 1894)**

www.mxpublishing.co.uk

Also from MX Publishing:

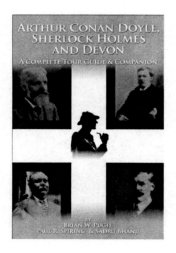

Brian W. Pugh and Paul R. Spiring

Arthur Conan Doyle, Sherlock Holmes and Devon

A Complete Tour Guide and Companion

www.mxpublishing.co.uk

Also from MX Publishing:

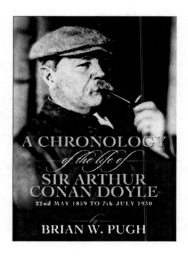

Brian W. Pugh

A Chronology of The Life Of
Sir Arthur Conan Doyle

A Detailed Account Of The Life And Times Of The Creator Of Sherlock Holmes

www.mxpublishing.co.uk

Also from MX Publishing:

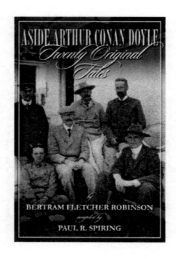

Paul R. Spiring

Aside Arthur Conan Doyle

Twenty Original Tales By Bertram Fletcher Robinson

www.mxpublishing.co.uk